APACHE ATTACK!

The bay horse, scenting the Apache ponies, neighed shrilly, and Bob Roberts, half rising from concealment, caught a glimpse of Manuelito's rag-bound head as the savages converged upon the thicket where the bay was hidden.

The Apaches, surrounding the bay in the manzanitas, read the signs, and grins spread across high-cheeked, flat-nosed faces. Here, written in the sand and brush, was a pleasing and humorous tale. One man had tied his horse in the manzanitas. The man had then left the horse and gone to the pile of boulders. The sign said so, and the Apaches, dispersing like desert quail—more silent than the quail hidden in the sand and rock and brush—slipped forward.

Bob Roberts waited among the boulders and wished he had a chew. His hand was beaten on the draw but he had to play it out; he had to stay, just on percentage, and because there was no chance to get away.

Other *Leisure* books by Bennett Foster:

THE MEXICAN SADDLE

GILA CITY

BENNETT FOSTER

LEISURE BOOKS   NEW YORK CITY

LEISURE BOOKS ®

September 2004

Published by

Dorchester Publishing Co., Inc.
200 Madison Avenue
New York, NY 10016

ISBN 0-8439-5387-X

The name "Leisure Books" and the stylized "L" with design are
trademarks of Dorchester Publishing Co., Inc.

Printed in the United States of America.

Visit us on the web at www.dorchesterpub.com.

Table of Contents

Foreword
by Patrice Williams

Bennett Foster had this to say about himself:

"I was born in Omaha, Nebraska in 1897. My father died when I was three and since then I've been brought up by various people: a grandmother, two aunts, three uncles, my sister, my stepfather, and my wife. I expect my three kids will eventually take over that job.

"In the course of the raising process I managed to live in a variety of places—Iowa, Illinois, Wyoming, and South Dakota, with brief interludes in other places. Also, in the raising process, I managed to go to school in Chicago and Wisconsin and graduated in 1921 from the New Mexico Agricultural College (now New Mexico State University), in Las Cruces where I had gone to run two farms for my uncles.

"Before graduating, I spent a couple of years in the Navy during World War I and found out that there was some country east of the Mississippi River. I've taught school, worked as a bacteriologist, done some engineering, fooled around a ranch or two, hired on with an entomologist as chief cook/bottle washer/grunt for a four-month pack trip to Arizona, have done some chemistry, clerked, farmed, raised some sheep, raised some cattle. Oh, you know—just fooled around.

"I like to fish and hunt. I like to bum in a car without any destination, and go until my money gives out. Since I can remember, I've been around cows and cowmen, some of whom have taken me under their wing and given me a liberal education concerning cattle, horses, guns, and their personal histories of the times.

"In 1930 I sold my first story to *West*—and it's been a typewriter from then on. I'll tell you why I like to write Westerns and why I think I can.

"First, I was raised in this country; I know it and the people that live in it.

"Second, I don't stay in one place. I move around out here, sort of circulate and ride grub line with my friends. The old salutation—'Light and rest your saddle.'—is about gone, but I find that—'Get out of your car and come in. We're just about to eat!'—is equally effective.

"I know how things ought to be done around an outfit. Maybe I can't do all of them myself, but I know how they should be done. I haven't any other interests. I always swore I'd run cattle and now I can run a bunch on paper and pick my crew from the boys I know.

"And finally I like to write Western stories because sometimes, when one of those old-timers has read a tale of mine, he will stare away into the distance, and his cigarette will hang loose in his lips, and he will drawl: 'That makes me think of the time. . . . Say, kid! How did you know about that?'

"And that, to me, is the final criticism."

Too old to be drafted, Foster signed up with the Army Air Force in World War II. At war's end, he was in India, processing men to come home from the Far East. When he himself came home to New Mexico in late 1945, he had to break into the writing business all over again. He was published by *Saturday Evening Post* and *Collier's* and *The Country Gentleman*. His published work totals nearly four hundred short stories and eighteen novels.

The Gila City stories have a single premise: an unlikely

combination of town drunkard and a more than slightly bent gambler set out to enrich themselves using some incident that has fallen into their laps. They are forced by circumstances to act contrary to their normal traits. The rewards are unusual.

Foster has a talent for imaginative plots and well-drawn characters. His own enjoyment of theses stories is obvious.

Mail for Freedom Hill

The buckboard carrying mail for Freedom Hill mining camp left Gila City at six on the morning of December 24th. It was a fine, cool morning, clear and cloudless, with a small wind blowing.

Several people saw the mail depart. Postmaster Jim Frazee was up, of course. The editor of the *Gila City Herald* and Dandy Bob Roberts, following an all-night poker game in the Mint Saloon, were eating breakfast in the OK Restaurant when the mail rattled past. Old Man Duggan, hostler at the livery barn, glanced through the dirty glass of the feed room window and glimpsed the buckboard start out for Freedom Hill.

On top of Carizzo Mesa, a half mile from town, Manuelito and another Apache buck watched. Manuelito dropped a handful of mesquite beans in the small, smokeless fire that burned between two rocks and, with the other brave helping, covered the fire with his blanket.

Al Simmons, driving the mail buckboard, was searching under the seat for his misplaced plug of tobacco and did not see the two white puffs of smoke that arose from Carizzo Mesa. Neither did anyone in Gila City, nor did they see the answering puff of white that lifted from Apache Wash, ten miles north of town.

The editor and Bob Roberts both looked up when Jim Frazee entered the restaurant. Frazee said—"Good morning."—sat down at the counter beside the two, and or-

15

dered breakfast from the night cook.

"I see you sent the mail out to Freedom Hill," the editor said. "Special trip, isn't it?"

"Kind of a Christmas present," Frazee said expansively. "I got Al to make the trip today in place of waitin' until Friday. Tonight's Christmas Eve."

The cook placed coffee and hotcakes in front of the postmaster.

"That's right." The editor revalued the item he had thought of when the mail rolled past. Mail to Freedom Hill at Christmas time was worth a story on the front page. "Was there much mail?"

"Not so much," the postmaster said. "Some of it's kind of important, though." As a public official, Jim Frazee was not one to hide his light under a bushel, and he liked to see his name in print. "There was stuff from the East, an' some local letters."

Mentally the editor composed his story: *Jim Frazee, our popular postmaster, arranged a special trip of the mail buggy to Freedom Hill this week. . . .* The editor shook his head, rejecting that lead. "So?" the editor prompted.

"Yeah." Frazee washed down a mouthful of hotcakes with a swallow of coffee. "I guess there's several people would like to know what was in the letter the assayer wrote Charlie Hoyte."

Dandy Bob Roberts glanced up from his plate. He had noted the departure of mail and wondered, professionally, if anything in the mail sacks was worth his while. Now he paid full attention to the conversation.

"D'you think Charlie's made another strike?" the editor asked eagerly.

"Could be." Frazee's tone and manner left no doubt as to his opinion.

Roberts frowned. Not more than ten days ago, riding on business of his own, he had seen Hoyte in a cañon in the Huaraches, north of Freedom Hill. He had thought at the time that Hoyte's burro was loaded heavily, but he had not investigated. Indeed, Roberts had taken pains to stay out of sight. It must have been ore samples that the burro carried.

"I was down at the commissioner's office yesterday," the editor said. "Charlie hadn't filed any new claims."

"Charlie," Jim Frazee announced, "don't file a claim until he knows what he's got. Remember when he hit the Little Boy Mine? He didn't file on that till he'd had an assay run. He sold the Little Boy to the Silver King people for fifty thousand. Charlie's smart. He don't want anybody cuttin' in on him."

"Wonder if Watson would tell me?" the editor speculated. Watson operated Gila City's assay office.

"You know he won't," Frazee scoffed. "Watson won't talk."

Old Man Duggan, accompanied by the odor of an early morning drink, stumped into the restaurant and sat down at the counter. Old Man Duggan was scowling.

Jim Frazee winked at the editor. "How are you, Duggan?" Frazee drawled. "Been fightin' any Apaches this mornin'?"

"I was fightin' Apaches when your mother was still pinnin' on your pants," Old Man Duggan growled. Then, to the cook: "Gimme some coffee!"

Dandy Bob Roberts got up, put a dollar on the counter, nodded to Frazee and the editor, and walked out. He did not want to hear Frazee and the newspaperman hurrah Old Man Duggan. That old liar was fair game for anyone and, with a drink or two, would tell long-winded stories of his exploits against the Apaches, all day long. Roberts wanted solitude, a little time, and, perhaps, his horse. If he could recall the location of the cañon in which he had seen Hoyte, and get there first. . . .

Roberts walked slowly along the sidewalk, under the wooden awnings that bordered Gila City's main street. He wished he could see the letter the assayer had written Hoyte. The assayer would talk to no one, particularly Roberts, but his report was in that letter. Knowledge of the assay report and a recollection of a cañon would be worth something. With that information a man could do pretty well for himself. He would not have to bother with such things as a marked card deck, a few calves lifted from the OYO in the Huaraches, or the pockets of a drunk in the alley back of the Mint. Dandy Bob Roberts headed toward his solitary adobe on the north side of Gila City. . . .

Three hours after the departure from Gila City, the mail buckboard returned, the sweating mules, ears flat against their necks, coming at a long lope. Simmons, lines loose in his lax hands, was keeled over in the seat, a feathered arrow shaft in his shoulder and a bullet burn along his right temple. There was a bullet hole in the seat, another in the tailgate, and three Apache arrows stuck upright in the buckboard bed. The nigh mule had an arrow graze on his left shoulder, and a flint arrow point was embedded in the collar of the off mule. The mules and buckboard wheeled into the safety of the Star Livery, where Old Man Duggan stopped them.

A crowd gathered quickly. Doc Speers came at a run from his office and directed the removal of Simmons from the seat. Simmons, weak from loss of blood, swore feebly and said that he had been jumped in Apache Wash. That was all the information the man gave; he fainted when Speers cut the clothing from his shoulder to probe for the arrowhead. Speers ordered an adjournment to his office, where he could work better, and four men, followed by a group of townsmen, carried the unconscious Simmons away. Old Man Duggan unhooked the mules and tied them in stalls, then went for the turpentine bottle, intending to doctor the arrow cut in the nigh mule's shoulder.

Dandy Roberts had gone to the Star Livery to get his horse when the mules came in. He wore a black hat with a rattlesnake band and a silver buckle. His cartridge belt was silver-studded, as was the holster of his .45; his boots were high-topped and new, and he wore a pair of silver-mounted, gooseneck spurs, big-roweled and with small chains dangling from the shanks. Dandy Bob liked fancy clothes and equipment. He had come honestly by his nickname.

He mixed with the men surrounding the buckboard and saw the three limp mail sacks under the seat. It was apparent that they had not been disturbed. Roberts itched to get his hands on the sacks, but there were too many others present. Especially Old Man Duggan.

Old Man Duggan backed out of a stall, the turpentine bottle in his hand. "Wisht *I'd* been a-drivin'," Duggan said. "Them Apaches wouldn't 'a' caught *me* asleep, igonnies! Look at that shotgun. Ain't been fired!" Brushing away the mail sacks, he picked up the weapon and broke it. The shells, bright and brassy, were undented by the firing pins.

"You!" Jim Frazee snorted. "If you'd 'a' been drivin', the mail wouldn't be in the buckboard. Apaches would be openin' it now an' your scalp would be hangin' from some buck's saddle."

Frazee was angry. His friend, Al Simmons, had been hurt. It had been the postmaster's idea to make the extra trip to get the Christmas mail to Freedom Hill. Old Man Duggan was harmless enough; he was drunk half the time and his stories of prowess against the Apaches were amusing. Ordinarily it was all right to kid along with Old Man Duggan, pretend to believe his yarns and inspire him to greater effort, but this was serious. A man was hurt and the mail was back in town and Old Man Duggan was still boasting. Frazee took the wind out of Old Man Duggan with swift, hard words.

"You damned old liar! Don't brag about what you'd have done. You never even *seen* an Apache."

From the door a man yelled: "Frazee! Al's come out of it an' is callin' for you."

Frazee turned to answer the summons. Old Man Duggan stared at the faces about him. "I've fit more Apaches . . . ," he began. The unbelief in the faces stopped him. Someone drawled: "Ah, hell! Shut up, Duggan. Nobody believes you." There was movement in the crowd as men filtered out of the livery barn, crossing the street toward Doc Speers's office. Presently only Duggan and Roberts were left.

"They think I'm lyin'," Old Man Duggan said slowly. "Why, damn them, they think I'm lyin'! Damn their dirty, rotten hides!"

"Ain't you?" Roberts asked.

"You know I ain't! I can take that mail to Freedom Hill right now! I c'n do it!"

Roberts shrugged. Old Man Duggan would boast and blow when he was in his coffin. He was a worthless old coot and his presence in the livery barn prevented Roberts taking the letter he wanted from the mail sack. Old Man Duggan would certainly give up head if the mail was tampered with. Casting one long and wishful look at the mail sacks in the buckboard, Bob Roberts walked past the vehicle and pushed open the back door of the barn. His saddled horse stood in the corral behind the barn. Dandy opened the corral gate, led his horse through, and, mounting, rode off, leaving the corral gate open.

Alone in the barn, Old Man Duggan stared at the buckboard, the open back door, and the rumps of the harnessed mules. Duggan had told his stories until he believed them himself. He had read the scorn on the faces about him when Frazee had voiced his opinion of the stable man.

Before Old Man Duggan stretched a bleak future in which no one bought drinks or listened to his tales of imaginary prowess, a future of derisive looks and slights that he dared not resent. Old Man Duggan reviewed that future briefly, and then went to the feed room. He emerged, carrying an almost full bottle from which he drank deeply. Then, putting the bottle on top of the mail sacks, Old Man Duggan backed a mule out of its stall.

He used an alley to leave Gila City. Well beyond the town he struck the road, and, with the mules trotting, he managed to set a fairly fast pace. As he drove, he fortified himself from his bottle, and his mind was as busy as the spinning wheels of the buckboard. He'd show 'em. He'd show 'em who could drive the mail. Every so-and-so in Gila City!

At Apache Wash, Old Man Duggan took a drink for luck before he crossed. On the far side he took another snort because his luck had been good. He pulled up Twelve-Mile Grade, the mules walking. He paused at the top to let the animals blow and, during that period, refreshed himself again. When the mules moved on of their own volition, Old Man Duggan was dwelling in a world of his own—and in which he was a hero.

Shortly after leaving the top of the grade, the old man began having trouble with his team. Mules and Indians are not sympathetic, and the critters that Duggan drove had already experienced bad times with Apaches that day. The wind blew from the north and the mules, catching the taint in that wind, laid back their ears and shied.

Old Man Duggan, rousing, straightened out his team and reached for the blacksnake whip under the seat. The mules shied again. Duggan poured on the leather—and the team stampeded. Frantic because of scent and whip, the mules laid their ears flat against their necks, clamped the bits in big yellow teeth, and legged it madly onward. . . .

Dandy Bob Roberts, riding north from Gila City, balanced one chance against another and made time, cutting across the loops of the road and saving distance. Roberts had remembered the location of the Huaraches cañon where he had seen Charlie Hoyte. Somewhere in the cañon there were prospect signs and small monuments marking claim boundaries. Roberts intended to find those markers and, having substituted notices of his own for those that Hoyte had left, hurry back to Gila City and file. The ethics of the matter did not bother him. He was fully able to hold the claim once he had filed on it.

There was, of course, the chance that he would not get to the Huaraches at all. A war party of Apaches was abroad. But Dandy Bob did not believe they would stop him. Having struck once, the Indians would shift their ground, he reasoned. And if they didn't, Bob Roberts was riding a good, grain-fed horse with a turn of speed. He could outrun any Apache pony. It was a chance for money against the chance of death that Roberts balanced. All over the Territory of Arizona, in those years, men balanced the two chances against each other and took the first. Dandy Bob was no exception.

He crossed the Apache Wash well east of the road and the site of Al Simmons's trouble. He rode up Twelve-Mile Grade, letting the bay horse take its time, his body easy in the saddle, big-roweled spurs gently brushing the bay's flanks, spur chains tinkling musically. Roberts nursed his horse and watched the country ahead, to either side, and behind. After the long climb up the grade he let the bay horse blow while he smoked a cigarette, then he struck out across country to where the road dropped down into Freedom Creek Valley before it climbed again. Bob Roberts had come fifteen miles and was halfway to Freedom Hill.

Four miles farther along on his journey, looking back, Roberts saw movement at the top of Twelve-Mile Grade. Reining the bay around, he studied the country. Now that the sun was high, heat waves were beginning to shimmer and distant objects were distorted, but Bob Roberts saw the movement again and determined its nature. The mail buckboard was crawling along the road!

Here was something unforeseen, an opportunity he had not believed would be presented. No one, certainly not Bob Roberts, would have believed that old blowhard, Duggan, would attempt to take the mail through to Freedom Hill. Roberts did not know of a man in Gila City foolish enough to make the attempt. But the buckboard was coming and in it was a letter Roberts wanted. Deliberately and very coolly Roberts prepared to take advantage of the chance presented him. If the mail buckboard failed to reach Freedom Hill the Apaches would be blamed—not Bob Roberts.

He rode along until a vantage point presented itself; a clump of boulders flanked by manzanita bushes by the road. Roberts tied his horse among the manzanitas and, with the rifle from his saddle scabbard, settled down in the nest of boulders. The view of the road was clear and it was not more than fifty yards away.

In that nest of boulders Manuelito and his companions found Bob Roberts. The Apaches were working at their trade, which was loot and murder. Whatever they could glean was grist for their mill and any lone ranch, any small party of whites, or single white man was fair game. The bay horse, scenting the Apache ponies, neighed shrilly, and Bob Roberts, half rising from concealment, caught a glimpse of Manuelito's rag-bound head as the savages converged upon the thicket where the bay was hidden.

The Apaches, surrounding the bay in the manzanitas, read sign, and grins spread across high-cheeked, flat-nosed faces. Here, written in the sand and brush, was a pleasing and humorous tale. One man had tied his horse in the manzanitas. The man had then left the horse and gone to the pile of boulders. The sign said so, and the Apaches, dispersing like desert quail—more silent than the quail hidden in the sand and rock and brush—slipped forward.

Bob Roberts waited among the boulders and wished he had a chew. His hand was beaten on the draw but he had to play it out; he had to stay, just on percentage, and because there was no chance to get away. He saw a movement to his right and below, watched closely, and then, squinting through his rifle sights, squeezed the trigger. A brown body rolled out from behind a rock, twitched convulsively, and lay still. Roberts's hand raced on the lever of the Winchester while, from right and left and straight ahead, shrill screams of anger arose.

The screams faded. Silence, filled with hate and anger, surrounded the boulders. Then through the silence came a rattle of wheels striking rocks, a pound of hoofs. Along the road, lurching and swaying, hat gone and with his beard blown by the wind of his passage, came Old Man Duggan and the mail for Freedom Hill.

The Apaches yelled again. About the boulders, squat, brown, breech-clouted men jumped to their feet. Arrows hissed and guns roared, and Bob Roberts, rising from the boulders, fired twice and, whirling, made for the road at a run. Above the yells and the clatter of the buckboard, a voice bellowed: "Whoa!"

The buckboard slowed and in that fractional second Roberts dropped the rifle and his clutching fingers caught the buckboard's end gate. The vehicle surged ahead but the grasp of those desperate fingers held. Roberts jumped and the springs of the buckboard sagged and swayed with the new load that struck the bed. . . .

It took the Apaches a little time to overcome their surprise and a little more to get their ponies. In that interval the mules and the loaded buckboard reached the downgrade to Freedom Creek. Also, in that space of time, Old Man Duggan had time to half turn and identify his passenger. Dandy Bob Roberts was seated on top of the mail sacks in the bed of the vehicle, clinging to the sides with both hands.

"You!" Old Man Duggan yelled. "If I'd 'a' knowed it was you, I'd never stopped."

Roberts did not answer but clenched his teeth against the jolting.

The Apaches, having retrieved their horses, were in no mood to quit their prey. The downgrade to Freedom Creek was a long slant. Manuelito led his braves to the lip of the hill, saw the buckboard careening down, and cut straight across, the two paths converging at the foot of the hill.

It was Old Man Duggan who first saw the Indians streaming down, but it was Dandy Bob who did something about it. Duggan yelled and Bob snatched up the shotgun Duggan had brought, cocked the weapon, and thumbed back both hammers.

The mules neared the end of the slope and once more shots sounded. An arrow buried itself in the seat beside Duggan. The head of a horse, sweat around the hackamore and flecks of foam on the jaw, appeared alongside Old Man Duggan. The horse pulled up level and Duggan saw a grinning, cruel face. He yelled and swung the blacksnake, and the lash cut the face and wrapped itself around the neck. The horse dropped back. In the back of the buckboard the shotgun roared. Old Man Duggan spared a momentary glance over his shoulder. Roberts had braced one foot against the side of the buckboard and was loading the shotgun.

"Watch your drivin'!" Roberts howled.

The Apaches had fallen back, checked momentarily by the shotgun blast. They came on again and Duggan, paying no attention to Roberts's order, watched them come. Pounding ponies drew up to the buckboard. An arrow struck Roberts in the arm as he raised the shotgun. The gun roared again. A pony went down, kicking and squealing in the road. Struck full and fair by a load of buckshot, an Apache brave with a dirty white rag around his head reeled back over the rump of his horse and was lost in the dust. Roberts dropped the shotgun and pulled out his Colt. His left arm was useless but his right still functioned.

The buckboard and its pursuers swept on across Freedom Creek Valley but the Apaches did not again push home a charge. Manuelito was dead and the others thought more of their skins than of scalps and loot. Old Man Duggan started the mules up the Freedom Hill grade, plying whip and voice to keep them running. The Apaches checked their pursuit at the bottom of the grade.

It was well they did. Halfway up the grade the mules played out. They stopped, heads low hung, sides heaving. Duggan turned to look at his companion. Bob Roberts was looking at Old Man Duggan. For a time they stared at each other, and then a slow grin broke under Duggan's beard and its fellow spread across Roberts's face. There was relief in the grins, and appreciation and, perhaps, comradeship.

"Well?" Old Man Duggan said testily.

"You come along about right," Bob Roberts stated.

Faintly, in the distance behind them, guns popped. "I wonder who they got after now," Bob Roberts said.

"It ain't us," stated Old Man Duggan with finality.

"No," Roberts agreed. "It ain't us, that's for sure. You done pretty well with that whip. I seen you hit that buck."

"You ain't no slouch with a shotgun," Duggan complimented. "Your arm hurt you?"

"It ain't comfortable," Roberts admitted.

Old Man Duggan wrapped the lines around a grab iron and hoisted his legs over the back of the seat. "Better fix it," he stated, dropping down beside Roberts. "I'm goin' to have to cut off them feathers so I can pull the arrer through."

The mail reached Freedom Hill at six o'clock on the evening of December 24th. By seven, when eight hard-faced citizens of Gila City, headed by Jim Frazee, rode in, the mail had been distributed. The Gila City contingent had been delayed *en route.* They had jumped a little bunch of Apaches in Freedom Creek Valley and had spent some time chasing brown-skinned will-o'-the-wisps among the rocks. It was dark when the men from Gila City dismounted in front of Freedom Hill's one saloon. They were tired and angry and, singly and collectively, had sworn vengeance on Old Man Duggan whenever they found him.

Vengeance was postponed. The first thing Frazee heard as he pushed into the saloon was Duggan's voice, high and crowing, like the pæan of a fighting cock.

"So here they come a-hellin', right alongside the buckboard. I hit one of 'em in the face with my whup an' I yelled to Bob. 'Let 'em have it, Bob!' I yells, an' Bob ups with the shotgun an' poured it to 'em. . . ."

Jim Frazee blinked his eyes in the light and stared. Here the important men of Freedom Hill were assembled. Burt Wheeler, manager for the Silver King; Pearl Baker, the city marshal; Karl Ochs of Ochs Mercantile; Dan Percival, who owned the saloon; Pat Hogan, owner of the Lucky Dollar Mine; and many another. They filled the saloon and, at the bar, Old Man Duggan and Dandy Bob Roberts formed the center of attraction. How Dandy Bob, upon whom all Gila City looked askance, had gotten into the picture, Jim Frazee did not know, but Dandy Bob was there.

It was Burt Wheeler who first spied the men from Gila City. "Here's the postmaster, boys!" Wheeler shouted, pushing through toward Frazee. "Here's the man who sent the mail up to us!" The manager of the Silver King caught Frazee's arm and pulled him toward the bar.

Within minutes every man from Gila City had a drink in his hand and found himself a hero, lesser only to Roberts and Old Man Duggan. Indeed, Jim Frazee stood only a rung below these two. Freedom Hill did not know that Old Man Duggan had stolen a buckboard, two mules, and the mail, and undertaken the trip on his own initiative. No, indeed! Jim Frazee received the credit for Old Man Duggan's drive.

At first Frazee was bewildered. The hilarity and the thumps on his back and the praise that poured upon him were confusing. Jim Frazee could not estimate the effects of mail at Christmas time, how men and women, isolated, cut off, in a savage desert country, would react to mail from home. He had built better than he planned when he loaded the buckboard that morning.

Mail for Freedom Hill, and Jim Frazee had wanted it delivered, but how could Jim Frazee know what was in the letters? How could he know about Burt Wheeler's Christmas bonus, or Pearl Baker's first granddaughter? How could he know that Percival had heard from the hospital and that Mrs. Percival would get well? Certainly Jim Frazee could not know that Pat Hogan had a letter from his mother in Ireland, or that Karl Ochs had a letter from his son, who was studying to be a doctor and who was coming home. But Jim Frazee did know that the back-slapping and the congratulations were pleasant and that the drinks were good.

"Yeah," Jim Frazee said. "I figured you boys would like to have your Christmas mail."

"Drink up, Jim. This one's on me."

At the bar Old Man Duggan told his story for the fifth time, embroidering it further. Beside Duggan, Bob Roberts drank in silence.

"C'm on, pardner," Old Man Duggan urged, his story finished, "have a drink."

Dandy Bob grinned morosely and threw his disappointment aside. "OK," he agreed.

Men left the saloon and others came to take their place as Freedom Hill celebrated Christmas Eve. Old Man Duggan told his story at least six times more, drinking as he talked. Gradually the crowd thinned. Men departed, some to their homes, others to collect their wives and children from the schoolhouse where there was a Christmas tree. At midnight only a few were left and Percival announced that he was closing for the night. Most of the men from Gila City had already gone in search of a place to sleep. Frazee found himself standing beside Charlie Hoyte.

"Get your letter, Charlie?" Frazee asked.

Hoyte tapped the pocket of his shirt. "Right here," he said. "It's a fine strike."

"Good, huh?"

Hoyte nodded. "You know," he said, "the day I struck this stuff, I spotted Bob Roberts watchin' me, up in the Huaraches. You know his reputation, Jim. For a while I thought maybe he had ideas about jumpin' my claim. I guess I was wrong."

"All right, boys, I'm closin' up," Percival called from the doorway.

"You might as well stay the night with me, Jim," Charlie Hoyte invited, putting his hand on Frazee's arm. "Come on." They passed through the door and reached the street.

"You know," Hoyte said, pausing to look back at the saloon while Frazee untied his horse from the hitch rail, "I think I'll cut Duggan an' Bob Roberts in on this strike I've made. There's plenty of it an' . . . well, they *did* bring the mail through."

"Yeah . . . but . . . ," Jim Frazee began.

"I'm goin' to do it," Hoyte announced, suddenly decisive. "I'll cut both of 'em in for a piece." Again his hand urged Frazee forward and the two men walked on down the street, Frazee leading his horse. They were out of sight in the darkness when Old Man Duggan and Dandy Bob came through the saloon door.

Dandy Bob had his good arm around Old Man Duggan's waist and his shoulder under the old man's armpit. Old Man Duggan's feet exhibited a tendency to stray.

" 'Let 'em have it!' I yells, an' Bob up with his shotgun an' poured it to 'em. Where we goin' to shleep, Bob?"

"In the buckboard, down in the wagon yard. Come on, Santy Claus."

"Shanty Claus!" The old man took umbrage at the term. "Shanty Claus yuhshef!"

"Come on," Roberts urged. He propelled Old Man Duggan forward.

Staggering a little, the men who had brought the mail to

Freedom Hill went down the street.

The night was fine and cool and starlit. The last of those who had gone to the Christmas tree at the schoolhouse were traveling home. Somewhere in Freedom Hill, voices were raised in song:

**God rest ye, merry gentlemen;
Let nothing you dismay. . . .**

The words came faint and clear through the night.

Christmas had come to Freedom Hill, and, although neither knew it, Christmas was just around the corner for Dandy Bob Roberts and Old Man Duggan.

The carol died away, and, in the silence that followed, the *clink* of Bob Roberts's spur rowels and the *tinkling* of his spur chains sounded, faint and clear and sweet and, somehow, vaguely reminiscent of sleigh bells.

Pilgrim for Boothill's Glory Hole

I

"THE PILGRIM"

The political complexion of Gila City changed at noon, one February day, when Tom Harmes met Frank McClintock. The meeting occurred on Main Street, and, when the echoes of the shots had died, Harmes stepped into the Mint Saloon. Frank McClintock, having stared unseeingly at the sun for a time, was loaded on a long shutter and taken to the warehouse back of Finebaum's store.

Gila City did things according to form. A coroner's jury rendered a self-defense verdict, and, as he left the inquest, Tom Harmes spoke to Sol Finebaum.

"Fix him up," Harmes directed. "Put a new suit of clothes on him an' get him a nice box. Charge it to me."

The gesture was not one of *noblesse oblige*. Harmes could afford it, for, with McClintock erased from the scene, he became the undisputed boss of Gila City, a position not without emoluments.

Naturally the town boiled with excitement. Men who had been lukewarm toward the Harmes faction hastened to declare their allegiance, while those who had backed McClintock made their plans either to join the winner or to leave town. Consequently, when the westbound stage arrived, only Old Man Duggan was on hand to witness the advent of the pilgrim.

The stage reached Gila City after dark. As hostler in the Star Livery, Duggan changed the teams, and, in the flurry of hooking up fresh mules and answering questions from the guard and the driver, the old man failed to see a passenger alight. Only after the stage had left was the pilgrim's presence made known.

A sharp—"I say, my man!"—brought Duggan up all-standing. There, on the stage platform surrounded by leather grips and gun cases, was a pink-cheeked, tweed-clad individual who leveled a forefinger.

"I say, my man," the stranger repeated. "Is there a hotel in the village?"

Old Man Duggan had never seen the like. He was both surprised and startled, but not too startled to talk. Never that. "There's the New York House," he said.

The stranger jingled coins in his pocket. "Will you show me there?"

Curiosity prompted the Old Man Duggan's subsequent actions. "Sure," he agreed and, stooping, burdened himself with two of the newcomer's grips. Duggan led the way while, carrying the rest of his baggage, the stranger followed.

In the lobby of the New York House the old man peered over the Savoy tailored shoulder while the register was inscribed: **Hon. Cecil Vivien Boyd-Smothe**. That was all Duggan waited for. He left the hotel and hurried down the street.

It was logical that Duggan should take the information to Dandy Bob Roberts. Dandy Bob and Duggan had been thrown together by circumstance when, despite a bunch of Apaches, they had taken the Christmas mail to the mining camp of Freedom Hill. Dandy Bob's part in the affair had been purely involuntary, brought about by his desire to appropriate a portion of the mail to his own uses. Duggan had been merely whiskey-brave. They had enjoyed a brief period of notoriety together and, since that time, Duggan reckoned

Dandy Bob his partner. The old man found Bob Roberts at the bar in the Rajah Saloon. Duggan was so excited that he forgot to cadge a drink.

"C'mon, Bob!" he ordered, seizing Bob's sleeve. "I got somethin' to show you."

"What's the matter with you?" Dandy Bob demanded, pulling free.

Duggan would not be denied. "C'mon," he urged, renewing his grip. "You got to see this."

Reluctantly Dandy Bob allowed himself to be dragged from the saloon. Matching his stride to the old man's eager gallop, he followed to the New York House, stopping on the porch. The Honorable Cecil Vivien Boyd-Smothe was still in the lobby, and Duggan thrust a gnarled finger against the door glass.

"Look-it!" he commanded. "See that pilgrim in there?"

Dandy Bob looked at the pink cheeks, the baggy tweeds, the deer-stalker's cap, and the blank expression of the pilgrim. "Well, what about it?" he asked.

"What about it?" Duggan fairly danced with impatience. "You see that in there an' you ask me what about it? Are you crazy, Bob? That there's a gold mine. You c'n play poker with him or deal him monte or sell him somethin', can't you?" The light of discovery burned in Duggan's eyes and his whiskey breath blew his straggling mustache.

Dandy Bob shrugged. "He's green, all right," he admitted.

"Green?" Duggan's voice went up a whole tone. "He's so green he makes grass look yeller. You remember I seen him first, Bob. I get halvers on him."

There was just one way to get rid of Old Man Duggan. Dandy Bob drew a half dollar from his pocket. "Get yourself a drink," he suggested. "I'm goin' home to bed."

Crestfallen, Old Man Duggan took the half dollar.

★ ★ ★ ★ ★

Frank McClintock was buried the next morning with most of Gila City attending the funeral. Following the ceremony Tom Harmes, ably assisted by Press Bell and Shorty Winn, his principal adherents, moved to establish himself in the kingdom his six-shooter had blasted. It was Press Bell who called upon Dandy Bob Roberts as that gentleman sat behind a solitaire lay-out in the Rajah Saloon.

Bell, tall and slab-sided, was reputed to be dangerous in a degree second only to his principal. He walked back and seated himself beside Dandy Bob.

"That red ten'll play on the jack," Bell stated, and as Bob placed the card: "Tom sent me over to see you."

"Nice of him," Dandy Bob commented.

"You ain't been around since that business yesterday." Bell disregarded Bob's tone. "Tom didn't figure that you were friendly to McClintock."

"I wasn't." Bob put a black nine on the red ten.

"Then why ain't you been around?"

Bob looked up from the deck. "I didn't see any reason to come around. McClintock's dead, so that's that. You was standin' in the door of the Mint, an' Shorty was across the street when Harmes an' McClintock come together. He had to watch three ways at once an' Harmes downed him. I didn't see no need to congratulate Harmes on that."

Bell scowled. "Kind of salty, ain't you?" he growled. "Mebbe you won't be so big when Tom gets his appointment as deputy marshal. You knew he was goin' to get one, didn't you?"

"I'd heard he might get an appointment."

"He's going to get it. An' he's goin' to organize things around Gila City."

"Yeah?" Dandy Bob put down the deck.

"Yeah. From here on Tom gets a cut on any deals around here. That's what I come to tell you. You can either throw in with us or pull out."

"Suppose I don't do either?"

Press Bell laughed, a mirthless bark of sound. "You saw what happened to Frank McClintock," he answered. "You got a reputation for bein' smart. Better come around an' see Tom." That was Bell's last word. He got up and walked out of the Rajah, speaking to the bartender as he passed. Dandy Bob sat motionless, the solitaire lay-out forgotten.

Bell's visit had forecast the future in Gila City. The town was due to be shaken down. The gamblers and the saloonkeepers and the proprietors of the houses along Poverty Row would pay Harmes for protection. And those other gentlemen, such as Dandy Bob Roberts, who made their living by an occasional speculation in other people's cattle, or who borrowed horses without permission, or relieved the stage of an express box, would also contribute. If they kicked in, they would be safe enough, but if they didn't, then Deputy U.S. Marshal Harmes would take them. And he would bring them in dead, no doubt about it.

Automatically Bob Roberts put the deck together and then stood up.

"Goin' out, Bob?" the bartender asked.

"I'm goin' to get my washin'," Bob answered. "I'll be back."

The Widow Fennessy was Gila City's official washwoman. Mike Fennessy, before his death, had operated the Limerick Girl, a small mine in the Bulton, north of town. Mike had never been a particularly good provider, believing that whiskey was more essential than food, and Mrs. Fennessy had taken in washing long before Mike's demise. Her house was at the edge of town, a quarter of a mile from the solitary adobe that Bob Roberts occupied.

Bob paid for his laundry and, having passed the time of day with Mrs. Fennessy, started home. He was still thinking about Press Bell's visit and was so engrossed that he did not hear his name called. Not until Old Man Duggan came panting up did Dandy Bob arouse.

"I been yellin' at you for a mile," Duggan admonished. "I looked all over for you."

"You found me," Dandy Bob stated tersely. "If you want to borrow money, you're wasting your time. I supported your last drink an' I ain't buyin' you another."

II

"LIMERICK GIRL"

Old Man Duggan waved the idea aside as being unworthy. "I don't want to borrow nothin'," he said. "I found out what that pilgrim is doin' in town. He wants to buy a mine."

"What's that to me?" Bob asked.

"Get a mine an' sell it to him," Duggan answered.

Bob Roberts laughed. "What mine would I get?" he asked. "There ain't a payin' mine that can be bought for less than fifty thousand, an' you know it."

Duggan brushed the objection aside. "Git one that ain't payin' then," he said. "Look here, Bob. This pilgrim come over to the livery today an' talked to Clyde. He's goin' to rent a rig an' I'm goin' to drive it for him. He ain't goin' to see nothin' but what I show him, ain't that right?"

Dandy Bob was facing Duggan and beyond the old man he could see the flapping clotheslines of the Widow Fennessy. An idea burst full-fledged into Dandy Bob's mind. "Listen," he said imperatively, "you take the pilgrim to the Holy Ghost an' the Turnbuckle an' the IXL tomorrow. Don't take him any place else."

"But them mines ain't for sale," Duggan objected. "You couldn't buy one of them."

"I know it," Bob interrupted. "That's why you'll take him to 'em. Tomorrow night you come around to my place. We'll get together an' I'll have a mine to sell him."

"Now you're talkin'!" Duggan exclaimed, his muddy eyes

gleaming their approbation. "An' don't forget. We go halvers."

"All right," Dandy Bob agreed. "We'll split."

"You better give me four bits now," Old Man Duggan suggested. "If we're pardners, I need a drink."

Bob Roberts, his eyes still on the widow's clotheslines, produced fifty cents from his pocket. "Go get your drink," he directed, "I've got business."

The Widow Fennessy was suspicious when Bob returned in so short a time. She was even more suspicious when he mentioned the Limerick Girl.

"Sure," the widow said when Bob broached the subject, "if it's the Limerick Girl ye want, ye're wastin' yere time. The vein's pinched out, an' there's no ore at all."

Bob Roberts knew that the Limerick Girl's vein had long been lost, and he said so.

"An' why do ye want it, then?" the widow demanded. "Ye're no miner, Bob Roberts. Ye don't think ye can find the vein when Mike couldn't . . . an' him lookin' for it, night an' day, for a month."

"It's a business deal, Missus Fennessy," Bob explained. "I want to buy an option on the Limerick Girl. I'll give you sixty dollars for an option. That's two dollars a day for a month."

This entailed more explanation. It took time to instruct the Widow Fennessy as to what an option was, and it took more time to get her to set a purchase price on the mine. Bob sat down and wrote out the option with a spluttering pen, and Mrs. Fennessy examined it.

"Sixty dollars is sixty dollars," she said, fingering the three double eagles Bob placed on the table. "An' all ye get is the right to buy the mine in wan month? If ye don't buy it, I keep the sixty dollars, an', if ye do buy it, ye give me a thousand more?"

"That's right," Bob agreed. "All you've got to do is sign that paper, Missus Fennessy, and you get sixty dollars."

The widow poised the pen. "That Tom Harmes wanted to buy the Limerick Girl wanst," she announced reflectively. "It was..."—she computed mentally—"four months ago. Just a month before Mike . . . God rest him . . . was kilt. Mike, bad cess to him, wouldn't sell, an' not a week after that he lost the vein an' there was no money at all."

"Just sign the paper, Missus Fennessy, an' you'll have sixty dollars," Dandy Bob insisted gently.

Still the widow poised the pen. "Poor Mike," she sighed. "He's been in Purgatory these three months now, with Father Rafferty prayin' for him. Right at the mine he was kilt, ye'll remember. The dirty spalpeens of Apaches shot him through the head, they did, but they didn't take his scalp. Wud Mike want me to sell the mine? I dunno."

"He'd want you to have the money," Dandy Bob answered.

"Little enough he gave me when he was alive." The widow became indignant. "Sure an' I'll sign it just to spite him."

She scrawled her name and Bob picked up the option while the widow tapped the end of the pen against her teeth. "I'll get the key to the shack," she said. "Ye'll want it. An' there's somethin' about the mine I shud tell ye. Somethin' poor Mike was tellin' me the night before he was kilt, but I misremember it."

Bob was impatient to get away. "You'd remember it if it was important," he assured. Much remained to be done and Dandy Bob wanted to see a man who worked in the Holy Ghost and was high-grading from the rich mine. For the project he had in mind Bob needed a small sack of high-grade silver ore.

The widow rummaged in the table drawer and produced a

key. "Here it is," she said. "Ye're welcome to it. An' I hope ye have good luck, Bob, an' buy the mine from me. If I had a thousant dollars, I'd start a boardin' house."

"Thanks, Missus Fennessy." Bob took the key. "I hope I pay you the thousand."

The next morning Bob rode out to see the mine upon which he had an option. The Limerick Girl was twelve miles out of town and there were no other mines near it. With a rifle on his saddle as insurance against the ever-present menace of Apaches, Bob sent his horse along at a good gait. He reached his destination and, reining in, surveyed the property. The Limerick Girl's dump and tunnel were halfway up a side hill above a cañon and in the bed of the cañon was the rock shack. Neither mine nor shack showed signs of having been molested and Bob dismounted and unlocked the shack door.

When he entered the small rock house, a pack rat ran scurrying, and Bob paused to brush cobwebs from his hat. Mike Fennessy had lived at the mine, coming to town only when he felt like it, and the shack was in disorder. There was a tangle of bedding on the bunk and under it a case of Giant powder. Tools, fuse, and the simple implements of housekeeping were strewn about and Dandy Bob grunted his disgust at the confusion. Methodically he set about straightening the place.

When he was done in the shack, he climbed to the mine dump. Here, according to reports, was where Mike Fennessy had been found, killed, so the finders said, by Apaches. Pausing briefly on the dump, Dandy Bob recalled a statement the widow had made. It was odd, he thought, that the Apaches had not scalped Mike Fennessy. Indians set a store by the hair of their enemies. But there was no accounting for the vagaries of Apaches and Bob shrugged. Advancing to the portal of the mine, he lighted a fat candle, brought from the shack, and then went in.

The tunnel reached back for about two hundred feet. Some fifty yards from the entrance there was a breaching tunnel, making a Y fork. Dandy Bob, as the widow had said, was no miner, but he had been around mining camps long enough to have some knowledge of the business. The branch tunnel, Bob surmised, had been driven in an attempt to find the vein of ore when it pinched out. Bob explored both tunnels, and then returned to daylight. As far as he could tell, the Limerick Girl was in shape to be sold.

Returning to the shack, he locked the door and started for town. Ore bodies, veins, and stringers were simply words to Bob Roberts. As far as he was concerned, rock was rock and there was plenty of it in the Limerick Girl.

Bob had fed his horse and cooked and eaten his solitary supper before Old Man Duggan appeared at the adobe. The old man, presaged by an odor of whiskey, was vastly pleased with himself. He had, as directed, taken the pilgrim to the Holy Ghost Mine, and there spent the day.

"Him an' Stevens got together," Duggan reported, "an' we never left the place. Stevens showed him all around."

"Did he buy the Holy Ghost?" Bob demanded anxiously.

"Naw. He couldn't. Stevens is only manager out there. He don't own the mine."

Thus reassured, Bob nodded. "So?" he prompted.

"So then we came back to town," Duggan continued. "The pilgrim's got a double-barreled rifle an'. . . ."

"Rifle?" Dandy Bob interrupted.

"That's what I said. A double-barreled rifle. It's big as a cannon. He says it's a tiger gun. We hunted jack rabbits with it clear up to sundown. When we got to town, he give me two dollars."

"An' you bought a pint!" Bob snapped. "I can smell it.

You're goin' to stay with me tonight, Duggan. I ain't goin' to have you gettin' drunk an' talkin'. It's already all over town that the pilgrim wants to buy a mine an' I'll bet there's ten men ready to sell him one."

"He ain't goin' to buy except from us," Duggan assured. "What did you git to sell him?"

"The Limerick Girl." Bob plunged into details, Duggan nodding now and then as he listened.

"Did you salt the mine?" he asked when Bob had finished.

"No. I'm no miner. I don't know how to salt a mine."

"You should've asked me." Duggan swelled with importance. "There ain't nothin' about minin' I don't know. Why, one time I. . . ."

"There ain't nothin' about nothin' you don't know," Bob broke in harshly. "Cut out the lyin' an' listen to me. I don't have to salt the mine. Here's what's goin' to happen." Rising, he walked to a corner and picked up a small sack.

"This is high-grade ore from the Holy Ghost," he announced as he placed the sack on the table. "An' here's an empty sack just like it. When you bring the pilgrim out to the mine tomorrow, I'll have these sacks in the shack. We'll put whatever samples he takes in this," Bob put his hand on the empty sack, "an', before you leave, I'll shift sacks. *sabe?*"

"Sure I *sabe,*" Duggan agreed. "But it would look better if you'd salted the mine. Ore is different from other rock, an' he might see the difference."

"He won't if he's as green as you say."

"He's green all right." Duggan's roving eye spotted a bottle on a shelf. "I think it'll work all right. Anyhow, we can try."

"An' we'll try tomorrow." Bob interpreted Duggan's glance. "You can have one drink an' no more. You're goin' to stay here an' you're goin' to stay sober till tomorrow mornin'."

* * * * *

Old Man Duggan, sleeping on the floor, rumbled peacefully throughout the night; Bob Roberts catnapped. Now, while he waited for action, he could see the holes in his scheme. He wished that he had salted the mine. Perhaps, as Duggan had suggested, the pilgrim would spot the difference between ore and native rock. And perhaps the pilgrim would bring Stevens, manager of the Holy Ghost, with him. If so, the whole plan was a failure. There were a lot of things that could go wrong and Dandy Bob, like an officer who has committed his troops, worried while he waited for the battle to begin. He roused at four o'clock, got the grumbling Duggan out of bed, then, having swallowed a meager breakfast, saddled his horse and started for the Limerick Girl.

Bob had a long wait at the mine. Duggan and the pilgrim did not appear until nearly ten o'clock. The old man halted the buckboard beside the rock shack and made the introductions.

"This here is Mister Roberts," Duggan informed the pilgrim. "I already told you about him gettin' hold of this mine an' wantin' to sell it. Mister Roberts is a cowman an' he ain't interested in keepin' the mine. This here is the Honorable Boyd-Smothe, Bob. He might buy your property."

Evidently Old Man Duggan had done some embroidery for the pilgrim's benefit. Dandy Bob extended his hand for the pilgrim to shake. "Pleased to meet you," Bob said.

"Charmed," the pilgrim drawled.

When Duggan and his passenger alighted, Bob saw a gun leaning against the buckboard seat. It was evidently the double-barreled rifle Duggan had mentioned.

"What kind of a gun is that?" Bob asked.

"A double express."

Old Man Duggan had no time for firearms. "It's a tiger

47

gun," he informed, "an' we're fresh out of tigers around here. What about the mine?"

"Ah, yes . . . the mine." The pilgrim adjusted his hat. "I'd like to look at it, you know. Mister Duggan has recommended it very highly. I'd like to take samples and so on."

"Whenever you're ready," Dandy Bob agreed, and led the way up to the dump.

They lighted candles at the portal and went into the mine. The pilgrim carried a small hammer and Bob the empty ore sack. Duggan hadn't lied when he said he knew all about mining, or else he had learned a lot overnight. He expatiated very professionally on the beauties of the Limerick Girl. At the fork of the tunnel the old man paused. Two tunnels, he said, meant twice as much ore, so making the Limerick Girl doubly valuable. Bob envied Old Man Duggan. He would never have thought of that explanation himself.

The pilgrim chipped small pieces of rock from various places in the tunnels and at the end of each took a number of specimens. It was at the end of the tunnels, so Duggan said, that the greatest values could be found. Presently they returned to the portal.

"I had a hell of a time gettin' him here," Duggan whispered to Bob when they had a moment alone. "He wanted to go back to the Holy Ghost."

"He ain't very interested," Bob said.

"That's the way he allus acts. He . . . ," Duggan broke off. "Yes, sir, Mister Boyd-Smothe," he said aloud. "What did you want?"

"I would like to see that second tunnel again," the pilgrim announced. "Twice as much ore, I believe you said?"

"Sure," Duggan agreed. "I'll take you right in."

III

"HAM-STRUNG TINHORN"

Duggan and the pilgrim went back into the mine, leaving the sack of samples on the dump. Bob Roberts seized the opportunity. Snatching up the sack, he hurried down to the rock shack where he made a swift substitution. When Duggan and the pilgrim returned from the interior of the mine, Dandy Bob, having some difficulty controlling his breath but feeling immeasurably better, was rolling a cigarette, and the sack of high-grade ore from the Holy Ghost was resting innocently against the timbering of the entrance.

The pilgrim picked up the sack. "I'll have these samples assayed," he said, "and, if they are as valuable as you say and Mister Duggan seems to think, I'll be definitely interested in your mine." The pilgrim took the path down from the dump. Duggan winked portentously at Bob before he followed, and Bob winked back. Each wink meant something different. Dandy Bob's wink meant that he had made the substitution and that everything was set; Duggan's that, having carried the freight so far, he would continue.

When they reached the rock shack, the pilgrim put the samples in the buckboard. As he did so, something moved in the brush on the slope opposite the mine. "There's a buck," Dandy Bob announced.

"A deer? Where?" The pilgrim seized his rifle and peered at the slope.

"He went upcañon. Maybe you can get a shot." Bob

pointed and moved at the same time. With the express rifle ready the pilgrim followed.

It was all very plain to Old Man Duggan. Bob was giving him an opportunity. When the pilgrim and Bob were out of sight, Old Man Duggan took the sample sack from the buckboard and carried it into the shack. There, where Bob had left it, hidden under the bunk, was the other ore sack. Duggan carried it out and placed it in the buckboard. Two shots sounded upcañon. Duggan grinned. There had been a deer after all. Presently the hunters returned, empty-handed.

"Git him?" Duggan asked.

"Missed the beggar," the pilgrim answered. "Just had a sportin' chance at him, y'know."

"That gun shoots a mile," Bob stated fervently. "The buck was clear at the top of the ridge, an' he kicked up rock under him with both shots. Runnin', too!"

"This is too heavy a rifle for small game," the pilgrim explained. "Only sighted for two hundred yards. Well, Mister Roberts," he climbed to the seat, "you'll hear from me. Good day."

Duggan clucked to the team and winked again at Bob. "So long," the old man said, and the buckboard went rattling down the cañon.

Bob was in no hurry. He did not want to pass the buckboard *en route* to town and so, going into the shack, he seated himself on the bed and rolled a cigarette. Presently, reaching under the bed, he pulled out the sack of samples and grinned at it. It seemed to Bob Roberts that his scheme was working.

There was no need to take the worthless samples to Gila City. Stepping to the door, Bob emptied the sack. A glint, as a piece of rock struck the ground, caught Bob's eye and he bent down and picked up the piece. It was almost pure horn silver. Bob's eyes widened. Surely the Limerick Girl did not . . . ? He knelt, picked up more bits of rock, and then swore luridly. Here were pieces of ore he recognized by peculiarities of shape and color. This was the highest grade ore that had come from the Holy Ghost. Dandy Bob rocked back on his heels and swore at length, realizing what had happened, knowing that, after he had changed the sacks, Old Man Duggan had changed them back again.

Nothing could be done about it. Bob might catch the buckboard, but he could not, under the pilgrim's eyes, make a substitution. The pilgrim was *en route* to the assay office with a bunch of worthless rock, and, when the report of what had happened leaked out, as it surely would. . . . Bob Roberts shuddered. He would leave Gila City before that happened. If he didn't, he would be laughed out of town. But before he left, he would have a word to say to Old Man Duggan!

Duggan, entirely satisfied with himself, kept up a running fire of conversation while *en route* to Gila City. The pilgrim was reticent. As they neared the town, Duggan's passenger issued an order. "Stop at the laundry, please, I have some clothing there."

Accordingly Duggan stopped at the Widow Fennessy's and waited while the pilgrim went in. The pilgrim was gone for some time, a much longer time than required by so simple a transaction as picking up a bundle of laundry. When he returned, he eyed Duggan curiously.

"Want to stop at the assay office?" Duggan asked.

"No. Go to the hotel," the pilgrim directed, "I'll not need you again today, Mister Duggan."

At the New York House the pilgrim unloaded and went in, carrying his laundry and the ore sack. Duggan drove to the Star Livery and unhitched. It was pay day, so, having drawn his money and with the pleasantly satisfied feeling of a man who has done a good job, he wandered down the street, entering the Mint Saloon.

The Honorable Cecil Vivien Boyd-Smothe, when he reached his room, put his laundry away and then sat down. As far as appearances went, Duggan's name for the Honorable Cecil was apt enough. He looked like a pilgrim, like a greenhorn. Actually he was anything but that. The Honorable Cecil was a mining engineer and a good one. Despite his youth he was the representative of a large British mining syndicate and he had worked in the mining districts of both British Columbia and the Transvaal. He was *en route* to the West Coast to take ship for Australia and he had stopped at Gila City to inspect the Holy Ghost and was writing a report. Only because of curiosity and Duggan's insistence had the pilgrim visited the Limerick Girl. Now he was intrigued.

Bob Roberts and Old Man Duggan were blatantly transparent. The Limerick Girl showed no ore at all and the pilgrim was curious as to how the mine had been salted, for he was certain that it had been salted. Moreover, when he had stopped for his laundry, he had mentioned the Limerick Girl and the Widow Fennessy had talked. The pilgrim was in possession of the facts relative to the mine, beginning with the loss of the vein and Mike's death, and ending with the sale of the option to Dandy Bob Roberts. The pilgrim opened the sack of samples and dumped the rock on his bed. His eyes widened for here were the samples he had taken. Surely Bob Roberts and Old Man Duggan did not think they could get away with this! They must have made some agreement with the assayer.

The Honorable Cecil considered that idea, then shook his head. Stevens, at the Holy Ghost, had spoken highly of Watson's integrity and the pilgrim's own observations at the assay office had borne out the report. And if the assayer was not in partnership with the two conspirators, something had gone wrong. They had made some mistake. The Honorable Cecil was curious and a gleam of humor appeared in his eyes.

He would, he thought, aid and abet the scheme, and, re-membering the Widow Fennessy and that she would get a thousand dollars if she sold the mine, the pilgrim made his plans. Going to a grip, he took out a canvas sack and emptied it into the ore sack that had contained the specimens taken from the Limerick Girl. The sack in the grip had contained specimens gleaned in the Transvaal and in British Columbia, jewelry rock, unbelievably rich, running thousands of dollars to the ton. Smiling and carrying his samples, the pilgrim left the room. When the assay report on these samples came in, it would show values such as Gila City had never dreamed. And, ostensibly, the samples came from the Limerick Girl.

Bob Roberts did not reach town until nearly sundown. His first stop was the Star Livery barn where he inquired for Old Man Duggan. The barn boss gestured toward the feed room. "In there," he said. "He's dead drunk. He got paid today an' I went in an' got him out of the Mint about half an hour ago." The barn boss grinned slyly. "I hear you been investin' in mines," he continued. "Think you'll sell the Limerick Girl?"

Bob Roberts did not answer. He kept his face straight while he cursed mentally. Old Man Duggan always talked when he got drunk, and this time, apparently, he had told all he knew. There was no use in wasting time at the Star Livery. Bob nodded to the barn boss and went home.

He had, of course, no way of knowing how much informa-tion Duggan had volunteered, and Bob certainly did not want to answer questions. He stayed at home that evening, drinking morosely and considering suitable punishments for his voluble partner. At midnight Bob went to bed, and, when he wakened, his head was as big as a washtub and ached intolerably. After three cups of coffee Bob felt a little better and decided that he would try to see Duggan again and straighten things out.

At the livery barn Bob learned that Duggan had gone out with the pilgrim. Whiskey never bothered Old Man Duggan—only the lack of it. Leaving word that he wanted to see Duggan as soon as he returned, Bob walked to the Rajah Saloon.

The place was deserted except for a bartender and, having indulged in a hair of the dog that bit him, Dandy Bob went back to one of the tables in the rear of the room. Gila City's weekly paper lay on the table and Bob read for a while. He was halfway through the paper when Tom Harmes and Press Bell came in.

Harmes and Bell came directly to the table and Bob put down the paper. The two seated themselves so that they faced him, and Harmes plunged immediately into the business of the meeting. "Old Man Duggan was in the Mint yesterday," he stated, "drunk an' shootin' off his head. He said you'd got an option on the Limerick Girl an' was goin' to sell the mine to this Englishman that's in town. How about it?"

There was no use in denying the facts. Dandy Bob nodded.

"The Limerick Girl is played out," Harmes said. "Fennessy lost the vein and was driftin' to find it when he was killed. I was interested in that mine once, so I know. Did you salt the mine before you showed it to this dude?"

"Yeah," Dandy Bob began, "but. . . ."

Harmes interrupted. "Press told you how things stood around here," he snapped. "We're in on deals like this an' you want to figure on it. We'll take a cut of what you get or else we'll go to this pilgrim an' tell him the mine's no good!"

There was combativeness in Harmes's voice and an answering antagonism arose in Dandy Bob Roberts. The bartender of the Rajah had come back to the end of the bar and was all attention. Harmes's threat did not mean very much to Bob Roberts. He knew, or believed he knew, that his scheme to sell the Limerick Girl was a gone goose anyhow. He was angry, he hadn't slept, and he had had enough of Tom Harmes. Dandy Bob got up deliberately and took a step back. Then, anticipating the men who faced him, he dropped his hand on his gun butt. Both Harmes and Bell were taken by surprise. They had not thought that Dandy Bob would make a two to one bet, nor had they believed that the conversation had come to a point where action was demanded.

"You," Dandy Bob snapped, "can go to hell, Harmes! You'll take no cut from me on anythin'!"

He was so utterly ready to back his talk, so sure of himself, that neither Harmes nor Bell dared accept the challenge. Dandy Bob Roberts was an uncertain quantity in Gila City. No one in town had ever seen him in action, but from all appearances he was proficient.

"Now, wait, Roberts." Harmes stared straight at Dandy Bob. "You're up against a proposition you can't buck. You know what happened to McClintock when he bucked me. He. . . ."

"You can find out how McClintock's gettin' along if you want to try," Dandy Bob interrupted. "You an' Bell ain't split up now, an' you forgot to bring Winn. I can see both of you at the same time. Now get out of here! You're maybe big enough to run Gila City, but you ain't big enough to run me! Get out!"

Harmes got to his feet. Press Bell stood up slowly. "You won't keep that mine, Roberts," Bell growled. "Mike

Fennessy thought that he. . . ."

"Shut up, Press!" Harmes snapped. "Go on out!"

Bell walked toward the door, Harmes following. Dandy Bob Roberts, stepping around the table, escorted them, keeping close to the wall so that he had the men at an angle. When Bell and Harmes were through the door, the bartender let go a long-held breath.

"I thought they wouldn't take it," he said. "You run it over on 'em, Bob, but you're a damned fool. They'll never let you get away with it!"

"I've got away with it so far anyhow," Bob answered as he went back to the table.

He seated himself against the wall so that he faced the door. Now that Harmes and Bell were gone he realized that what he had done was dangerous. The bartender was right. Tom Harmes could not afford to let Dandy Bob stay alive, not if he expected to run Gila City. Recalling the events as they had occurred, Bob wondered at himself. He had been, he thought, a little crazy. He thought another thing. Bell had started to say something about Mike Fennessy and Harmes had shut Bell up. Bob recalled how the Widow Fennessy had said that Mike had not been scalped. With the recollection came certainty. Apaches had not killed Mike. Mike had refused to sell the Limerick Girl to Harmes, and Harmes had killed him. Of course, Dandy Bob could not prove this, but he was very, very sure. Else why had Harmes shut Bell up?

A sudden darkening of the door roused Dandy Bob and he straightened only to relax again. Old Man Duggan was in the doorway, peering into the room, and behind Duggan was the pilgrim.

"There you are!" Duggan half shouted in his excitement. "I been lookin' every place for you!" He bore down on Dandy Bob, the pilgrim following. "We got that assay report,"

Duggan announced as he halted. "Look at it!"

Bob took the paper the pilgrim extended. The pilgrim's eyes sparkled but his face was expressionless. Dandy Bob read the figures on the report. According to the assay the Limerick Girl gave values amounting to $24,000 a ton in gold and $9,000 a ton in silver. Bob read the figures again, then, looking up, he stared at the pilgrim.

"A very fine report, Mister Roberts," the pilgrim said. "Naturally I am interested in the mine."

Bob could tell nothing from the pilgrim's face. He looked at the report again. Values such as these had never been seen in the Gila City district, particularly the gold values. Gila City was a silver camp. There was something wrong with the report, something very fishy. Once more Bob looked at the pilgrim.

"That's a good report," he drawled. "Better than I expected. I want to look at the mine again before I talk about sellin' it."

A glint of respect shone in the pilgrim's eyes. This was a development he had not foreseen. The pilgrim had planned to lead Bob on until he had taken up the option and paid the Widow Fennessy her thousand dollars. Then, preferably in front of a crowd, the pilgrim intended to call Bob's hand and tell the story of the salting of the Limerick Girl.

"Ah, of course." The pilgrim's drawl matched Dandy Bob's.

Duggan could not understand what was happening. He was sure that Bob was insane, and, for once in his life, the old man was stricken dumb.

Bob returned the assay report. He was thinking rapidly and clearly. There was a showdown due between himself and Tom Harmes, and Bob was not foolish enough to believe that the deck would not be stacked. Bob did not want to avoid the showdown, but he did want an even break, better if he could get it. He did not wish to do as Frank McClintock had done, walk into a set-up from which there was no escape. In Gila City, with all the Harmes faction on hand, Bob would be trapped. But there was no need for a showdown in Gila City. Bob could pick his own ground. A man in a mine entrance had only one way to look and one spot to watch. The Limerick Girl had offered that advantage. Also, there was just a chance that the assay report was correct, that untold values lay in the Limerick Girl. Bob did not think so, but he was not sure. He intended to find out.

"I'll see you after I've looked at the mine again," Bob told the pilgrim. And then, turning to the bartender: "I'm goin' out to the Limerick Girl. I'd like Tom Harmes to know that an' to know that I'll be lookin' for him out there." Paying no attention to Duggan, the pilgrim, or the bartender, Dandy Bob walked out of the Rajah.

IV

"ATTACK"

He was cautious on the way to his adobe but saw nothing of Harmes or Bell or Shorty Winn. When Bob reached his house, he packed food into a gunny sack, filled a big canteen with water, and checked his supply of shells for the Winchester. He did not think that he would have to stand a siege, but he wanted to be ready for one. He saddled his horse under the shed, where he had only the front to watch, tied the provisions and canteen to his saddle, and, with his rifle in its scabbard, rode out of town, glad that he had but a short distance to go to reach open country.

Arriving at the Limerick Girl, Bob staked his horse in the cañon where he could see the animal from the mine entrance. The horse would act as a sentinel, becoming alert at the approach of other horses. Then, laden with his supplies, Bob climbed the path to the entrance. He had chosen his ground and position.

An hour passed and half of another. Dandy Bob made brief excursions into the mine but dared not remain away from the entrance for any length of time. At the end of the hour and a half Bob's horse lifted its head and nickered. The sentinel was on duty. Bob picked up his rifle, and Old Man Duggan, mounted on a livery stable horse, rode into sight.

The old man left his mount with Bob's and toiled up the slope to the dump. No one in Gila City, with the possible exception of the minister, was without firearms and Duggan did

59

not break the rule. Arriving on the dump, he grounded the butt of his double-barreled shotgun and, when he had recovered his breath, addressed Bob.

"Of all the damned fools! Why didn't you sell to the pilgrim? If ever I seen a man ready to buy a mine, he was it. Are you loco, Bob? What did you want to buck Tom Harmes for? Why didn't you cut him in?"

"Because I've got a bellyful of Tom Harmes," Bob answered the last question first. "An' because there's somethin' fishy about that assay report. That report was made on the samples the pilgrim took right here in the mine. I changed the sacks an' then you changed 'em back."

"The hell!" Duggan could not believe what he heard.

"That's right," Dandy Bob assured. "Either the pilgrim salted those samples or the values are in the mine." Briefly he detailed events of the previous day for Old Man Duggan.

"You dumped that other sack by the house?" Duggan asked when Bob had finished.

"That's right."

"I want to see," the old man said. "If you're right, that report was made on what come from the mine. The pilgrim's too damn' green to do any saltin'."

"I ain't so sure he's green," Bob replied, "but you're welcome to look. Only watch out. I'm expectin' company."

"Harmes," Duggan growled. "Damn him! He ain't goin' to get any cut. We got a mine here."

"Maybe."

Duggan went down the path again. He was gone for some time, and, when he returned, he was loaded like a pack mule. Besides the shotgun, Old Man Duggan carried drills, a jackhammer, a shovel, and his shirt front bulged with a covered load. "I'm goin' into this here mine an' take a sample from every damn' foot of it. We'll have 'em assayed ourselves, an' then we'll know what we got."

"Help yourself," Bob invited.

Duggan went into the mine. Bob rolled and lighted a cigarette and watched the horses, occasionally shifting position so that he could sweep the hillside with his inspection. He could hear Old Man Duggan back in the mine. There was an indistinct muttering as Duggan held conversation with himself. From the tone Bob judged that the talk was profane. Occasionally a hammer *clinked* against rock as samples were taken. Then, from far back in the mine, came the steady *ring* of steel against steel. Evidently Duggan was using the jackhammer on a drill. Time wore away and the hammering ceased. Dandy Bob hardly noticed for, in the cañon, the two horses had lifted their heads and were watching intently.

"Roberts!" Tom Harmes shouted from downcañon.

"Yeah?"

"Just wanted to make sure you was here. You can come down from your perch an' take it, or we'll blast you out."

"Go on an' blast." Dandy Bob did not need the horses now. He had Harmes located. "It'll take you a while."

A laugh echoed against the cañon slopes. Bob looked up quickly, just in time to catch a flurry of movement on the hillside opposite the mine entrance. Following the laugh there came a report and lead shattered rock at the tunnel mouth. Dandy Bob stepped back quickly, halting just inside the entrance of the Limerick Girl. It dawned upon him suddenly that this battleground of his choosing was not without faults. He had been watching the cañon floor and either Press Bell or Shorty Winn had slipped into position opposite the mine, commanding the entrance. A second rifle spoke and lead struck at a new angle. Dandy Bob ducked and cursed. Both Bell and Winn were across the cañon and they had him euchered!

"Still feelin' pretty good?" Harmes called jovially. "Kind of hot up there, ain't it?"

Bob stayed close to the left wall and searched the opposite slope for a target. He did not answer.

"Step out an' we'll settle it!" Harmes called. His voice was nearer, coming from below the dump. "I'll call off Press an' Shorty an' we'll take our chances."

"Like Mike Fennessy took his," Bob replied, sarcasm in his tone. "I've got a picture of you takin' chances, Harmes."

"Fennessy was a bull-headed damned fool." Harmes had come even closer. He was directly below, hidden from the entrance by the dump. "He was as bad as you are. I had to kill him. Are you comin' down, Roberts?"

A foolish question. Dandy Bob answered it by shooting at a movement across the cañon. Press Bell called: "Missed me a mile, Bob!"

There was a scrambling sound behind Bob. He half turned. Old Man Duggan was running along the tunnel toward him. "Fire in the hole!" Duggan shrilled. "Get out, Bob!" Dandy Bob seized Duggan's arm. The old man tugged to free himself. "Fire in the hole!" he repeated. "C'mon! C'mon!" The old man jerked free, started to run again, and rock, chipped from the wall by a shot, splintered into his face. Duggan dropped flat on the tunnel floor. A great, forceful hand seemed to lift Bob, picking him up and slamming him forward. He was spewed from the tunnel mouth, flung across the dump and, his rifle lost, went rolling down its slope.

Across the cañon, Shorty Winn and Press Bell, taken by surprise by Bob's sudden appearance, gathered their wits sufficiently to fire once each. Both missed. Bob, half stunned, landed at the bottom of the dump and was temporarily hidden by brush and rocks. He scrambled to his feet and, as he reached them, Tom Harmes came into view, six-shooter in his hand, not fifteen feet away. Harmes, too, was surprised and there was a fraction of time before he recovered. Then, leveling his gun, he fired.

The shot burned Bob's neck. His hand, moving almost without volition, swept back to his side. The Colt was still in its holster, jammed tight by the fall. The gun came down and, across that short distance Bob Roberts's first shot blended with Harmes's second, beating it by a fraction. Harmes lurched and then, as Dandy Bob's second shot struck him, reeled back and went down, pole-axed by the impact of the two heavy slugs. Dandy Bob, bruised and battered by his fall, clothing torn, limped toward the man he had killed.

The movement exposed him to the riflemen above. Press Bell stood up to get a better shot, and Old Man Duggan, wits and shotgun both recovered, let go a double-barreled blast. Bell squawked and dropped his rifle as buckshot tore his cheek. He lost his footing and came rolling down, bringing up against a scrub cedar where he lay motionless.

From farther down the cañon a gun bellowed in two quick explosions. Shorty Winn, yelling his fright, broke from concealment and ran. Again came the two explosions, one on the heels of the other, and Winn increased his speed, threshing through the brush until he reached the top of the ridge and disappeared. Silence settled on the precincts of the Limerick Girl.

Old Man Duggan broke the silence. His shotgun clutched across his chest, he peered over the edge of the dump and spied Dandy Bob. Duggan's voice quavered.

"What happened, Bob?"

"Damned if I know." Dandy Bob had satisfied himself that Harmes was dead. Never again would Tom Harmes declare himself in on the happenings around Gila City. "What did you do in the mine?" Bob looked up at Duggan. "An' who was that shootin' down the cañon?"

The last question was answered immediately. "I say, you chaps!" a voice called. "I say, I'm a friend, y'know. Don't shoot."

"The pilgrim!" Dandy Bob and Duggan exclaimed simultaneously.

"Come on in!" Dandy Bob shouted his answer to the pilgrim.

There was a pause, broken by sounds of progress over rock. The pilgrim, bearing his double express rifle, appeared. Duggan came scrambling down from the dump and the pilgrim halted. "Not sportin'," he stated. "Not sportin' at all. Three against two. I took a hand and joined the fun, but I missed the rascal. Must get this gun sighted for longer distances. I really must!"

All three turned as rocks rolled above them. Press Bell, who had been stunned by his fall, was scrambling up the slope. Duggan threw his shotgun to his shoulder but Bob's sharp—"Let him go!"—stayed the old man's finger on the trigger. They watched Press Bell out of sight.

When Bell had vanished, the three men went to Tom Harmes. As they looked at him, Dandy Bob spoke. "He killed Mike Fennessy. He said so. It wasn't Apaches that killed Mike, like they thought." Somehow it seemed important to Dandy Bob to make the statement. Not that Mike Fennessy's death entered the matter in hand, but Bob wanted the others to know the truth. Perhaps a sense of justice and retribution made him speak so.

No one said anything for a moment. Then Duggan growled: "He's dead himself now. He asked for it an' he got it."

Again a silence. Dandy Bob broke it. "What happened in the mine?" he demanded. "What did you do, Duggan?"

Duggan scratched his head. "I dunno," he said. "I took a bunch of samples an' I wanted to get some real ones from the face. I drilled a hole an' loaded it an' lit the fuse. Then I heard the shootin' an' yellin' an' I tried to put the fuse out but I was too late so I run. The whole damn' mine exploded. I'd loaded the hole light, too."

"Suppose we go and see," the pilgrim suggested.

They climbed to the mine and, having lighted candles, went in. At the branching of the tunnel there was a mass of fallen rock. Duggan and Dandy Bob went on, back to the end of the main shaft, but the pilgrim paused.

At the tunnel end, there was a small amount of loose rock and Duggan examined pieces. "No ore here," he said. "Not a sign of it. Bob, I dunno."

"Let's get out," Bob said.

Retracing their steps, they met the pilgrim coming toward them. His coat sagged with additional weight, but neither Bob nor Duggan noticed. "We're goin' back to town," Bob informed. "We've got to catch our horses an' we've got to take Harmes in someway."

"I came out in a buckboard," the pilgrim said diffidently.

"Then we can take him in that," Bob stated.

It took time to catch the horses and for the pilgrim to get the buckboard into position. When Harmes's body was loaded, all three men crowded onto the buckboard's seat, Duggan assuming the lines as though by right. The loose horses had been tied to the hames of the team and so they started back to town.

The body, covered by a blanket from the shack, was a depressing influence, but nothing could keep Old Man Duggan still for long. By the time they had cleared the mouth of the cañon and were on the road to town, Duggan was talking. He spoke frankly, apparently forgetting that the intended victim

65

of the hoax rode beside him. Old Man Duggan swore that there was no mineral in the tunnel of the Limerick Girl. "I don't give a damn what the assay run," he said. "That there's rock an' nothin' else. I know. I been minin' long enough. I ought to."

"You mined like you fought Apaches," Bob scoffed. "I'll know what's in the mine when I see an assay on samples I've taken myself."

The pilgrim cleared his throat apologetically. "About that assay," he said. "I'm afraid I pulled your leg there. I'm a mining engineer, y'know, and, when I saw how eager you chaps were, I wanted to help you out as best I could."

Duggan and Bob stared incredulously at their companion. "Then you . . . ?" Bob Roberts began.

"I had specimens from the Transvaal and from British Columbia in my grips." The pilgrim nodded. "I substituted them. Really, I'm not so green, y'know. I've been around a bit."

That statement put a stopper on even Old Man Duggan's clacking tongue. He just blinked his eyes.

It was dusk when the buckboard halted in front of the Star Livery. Within minutes a crowd gathered. Jim Frazee, the postmaster, Al Simmons who drove the mail buggy, the justice of the peace, the constable, Watson the assayer, Stevens from the Holy Ghost mine, most of Gila City assembled about the buckboard, and, at the edge of the crowd, was the Widow Fennessy. She stood with her hands on her broad hips.

The pilgrim told the story. Vouched for by Stevens, the pilgrim was the center of attraction, and, when he had finished his brief recounting, there was no doubt in the mind of any listener but that Dandy Bob was clear. It had been a fair fight at the finish; Bob had shot in self-defense. And the pilgrim added a touch when he spoke of Harmes's killing Mike Fennessy.

Dandy Bob answered questions, filling in the gaps of the pilgrim's story. "Duggan touched off a blast," he said. "It was a light shot, but someway it blew me out of the tunnel. I. . . ."

"Praise the saints, I remember now!" the Widow Fennessy's voice shrilled as she pushed her way through the crowd. "That was what Mike was tellin' me. He'd put shots in the new tunnel an' some of them didn't go off. He was cursin' an' swearin' about it, sayin' how dangerous it was."

"And when Duggan's shot fired, the others exploded," the pilgrim explained. "That's what happened." He looked at the assembled townsmen and smiled.

"Anyhow I got blowed out of the mine," Bob Roberts said ruefully. "An' the mine's no good."

"I'm not so sure of that," the pilgrim said quickly. "That second tunnel, y'know. I investigated that a bit. Picked up a few specimens. I believe there's quite a body of ore." His hands delved into the pockets of the sagging coat and brought out bits of rock. "I'd like your opinion," he completed, handing specimens to Watson and Stevens and then stepping back.

In the light streaming from the livery door the assayer and the manager of the Holy Ghost examined the samples. "It looks like our ore from the Holy Ghost," Stevens said slowly.

"Pretty good stuff, I'd say," Watson announced cautiously. "Of course, I'd want to run an assay." He pulled at his nose and then rubbed his jaw.

"There's quite a large deposit," the pilgrim announced blandly. "The explosion brought down part of the roof and the ore is above. Quite valuable."

Duggan pinched Dandy Bob's arm. Dandy Bob's thoughts were those of the old man. Bob had an option to buy the Limerick Girl in his pocket, and the option had almost a full month to run. One thousand dollars was the purchase price, and, if the pilgrim was right, there were many thousands of dollars to be taken from the Limerick Girl. It looked good for Dandy Bob Roberts.

The pilgrim's next words blasted Dandy Bob's plans. "Of course," he said calmly, staring at Dandy Bob, "this alters matters, don't you think? Your option from Missus Fennessy was taken when the mine was worthless. I'd tear it up if I were you. Only sportin' thing to do." The pilgrim's eyes never left Bob's face.

Every eye was on Dandy Bob. At that moment he could have killed the pilgrim. Under the eyes of Gila City he could not but take the suggested action. Slowly reaching into his pocket, he brought out the option and his reluctant fingers tore it across, once and then again.

As the pieces of paper fluttered to the ground, the Widow Fennessy squealed. "Ye're my pardner, Bob." She clutched Dandy Bob's arm. "Half the mine's yere's." Her big body shook with delight.

"No." Dandy Bob shook his head. "It's all yours, Missus Fennessy." His brain felt a little numb.

"Quite right." The pilgrim's voice was crisp. Then, having carried his point, the tone softened. "And now," he said, "I'll buy a drink. I believe that's the proper expression, isn't it? Drinks all around for the crowd?"

"That's right." Old Man Duggan seized the pilgrim's arm. "Sure. Let's go to the Rajah. It's closest." Duggan urged the pilgrim forward and, as they moved, so too did the crowd. Dandy Roberts hesitated and then fell into step behind Duggan and the pilgrim. He eyed the erect back of the Honorable Cecil Vivien Boyd-Smothe and scowled, and, as he scowled, he muttered: "Pilgrim. Pilgrim, hell!"

Dandy Bob's
Cold-Deck Cattle Deal

I

"DANDY BOB COMES HOME"

•

There was no wind and the westbound stage from Tucson was shrouded by the dust of its own passage. Dust, fine and impalpable, surrounded driver, guard, and coach. It filtered up through the floorboards and seeped through the cracks about closed doors and windows, filling the interior and settling on the passengers.

There were three passengers. Two, on the front seat, were commercial travelers, neat men, well-dressed, heavy watch chains curved across their well-filled vests, shoe-shod feet braced against the middle bench. They whiled away the time with tobacco and conversation. The third man slept, sprawled out, occupying all the back seat, black hat tilted to cover his eyes, mouth opened a little, snoring gently, body relaxed and lurching with the sway of the coach on its leather thoroughbraces.

"Roberts!" The smaller of the two drummers rolled his cigar between his lips and eyed the man on the back seat. "Dandy Bob Roberts. The city marshal puts him on board at Tucson, moves us over here where we have to ride backwards, and gives him all the back seat where he promptly goes to sleep. I think I'll wake him up."

The second salesman, older and wiser, grinned sardonically and shook his head. "Your first trip in this country, ain't it?" he asked. "After you've made this territory a time or two, you'll know more. You notice *I* didn't complain about being

71

moved. I shuffled over here like a good little boy. And I don't think you'll wake him up. He'd eat you alive if you did."

The small man snorted contemptuously, and the larger spoke again. "I mean it," he warned. "I know the breed. He's a gambler and gunman. Probably killed a man or two. When he wakes up, I'll try to interest him in jewelry. Maybe give him one of my samples. Get a man like that to wearing one of our new, patented, guaranteed watch guards and half the men in Arizona Territory will want one. You'll see how I'll handle him."

Dandy Roberts snorted suddenly, clearing his nostrils of dust. Both drummers jumped and then relaxed as he resumed his gentle snoring.

From his high seat over the front boot the driver spat through the dust toward a soapweed. "Walnut Springs next," he said. "Then twelve more miles to Gila City. I think I'll wake up Bob at Walnut Springs. He'll want to clean up some before he gets to town."

The guard, young and hard-faced, a shotgun across his knees, nodded. "An' I'll give him his gun," he agreed. "The marshal said not to give it to him until Gila City, but Walnut Springs is close enough." He pulled a walnut-handled Colt from beneath his leg and looked at it. "I wonder if this is the gun he used on Tom Harmes?" the guard said.

"Likely." The driver spat again. "Bob wears fancy clothes, but when it comes to tools, he's plumb practical. You wouldn't see him carryin' a gun with pearl or ivory grips. Too apt to slip. Funny thing about Bob. Every year he goes up to Tucson an' gets a lot of new duds. Best-dressed man in the territory, I guess. Did you see that big package Abe Meyer put on for him? Them are all new clothes."

The guard still fondled the Colt. Guns were his obsession and his livelihood. "Bob must've throwed a real one in

Tucson," he commented enviously. "I heard he run up a stake of five thousand in the Tivoli an' then spent it all last night. Guess the Tucson police was glad to get him out of town."

"They're always glad," the driver agreed. "You can't tell what a man like Bob Roberts is goin' to do. I mind one time. . . ."

The six horses were toiling up a grade and momentarily the dust lessened. From a cluster of rock and mesquite a shot sounded, hard, flat, vicious. The guard, half rising from his seat, dropped the walnut-handled Colt and lurched forward, his shotgun sliding from his lap. For an instant he seemed to hang suspended, and then pitched down, over the dash, between the frightened wheelers. The driver, his hands full of leather, hauled back on the lines and jammed his foot against the brake, fighting to quiet the plunging teams.

"Whoa! Whoa, now!"

Brake, lines, and voice had their effect. The stage ground to a stop. From the mesquite, level with the stage now, came a second shot, splintering the wooden frame at the top of the door.

Inside the coach, Dandy Bob Roberts came alive as the first shot sounded. Before the stage stopped he was crouched by the bench, his hand reaching for his holster, finding it empty. He remained crouched and, when the second shot plowed through the top of the door, snapped fiercely at his companions. "Down! Get down!"

The big man crouched obediently, but the smaller man, wild with panic, reached for the door. Bob thrust him back into his seat.

Now a voice sounded, muffled by closed door and windows. "Get your hands up, there on top. Passengers stay inside an' you won't get hurt."

The smaller man quit struggling, and Bob let him go. He

73

risked a look through the window. Desert, nothing else, met his eyes. Dandy Bob dropped back on the leather cushion of the seat. "You'll be all right," he assured his companions. "He's just after the express box."

Shouted directions and the swaying of the coach marked the progress of the hold-up. The technique, Bob thought, was good. Remembering other occasions, he judged that there was just one man working. Two men would have hailed the passengers forth, lined them up, and relieved them of their valuables. The first shot had dropped the guard, that was certain; otherwise, there would have been a fight. The driver, hired to drive and not for combat duty, offered no resistance other than verbal. According to the ethics of such affairs, drivers were allowed to curse bandits, and this driver did. Bob heard him as the express box *thumped* down into the road.

"Now clean out the boot," the hold-up man ordered. "Throw down grips an' boxes."

"My samples!" The big traveling man half rose. "Jewelry!"

"Shut up!" snapped Dandy Bob.

Abe Meyer, Tucson's Bon Ton Tailor, had labored long and assiduously. In Bob's luggage were a new Prince Albert coat, three pairs of trousers, and four vests, all tailored to his measurements. He had hoped that the bandit would neglect the contents of the boot, but no such luck. The stage rocked as the driver toiled.

"Damn you," he said. "That's all of it."

"Then cut off your first two teams. You can get along with the wheelers."

The driver swore again, luridly and at length. "You killed Mike, an' now you're tryin' to get us all killed. There's Apaches, an'. . . ."

"Unhook them horses!"

A *clink* of metal sounded as tugs were unhooked. Horses moved.

"Now are you satisfied?" the driver demanded sullenly.

"Load in your pardner an' pull out."

There was a pause, then the door opened. The driver, carrying the guard, appeared in the opening and Bob Roberts, reaching out, laid hands upon inert flesh, and pulled. The guard rested on the middle bench, dead, a wound in his head, a great big hole. The door slammed shut, the coach rocked, and then the whip *popped*.

"Git up. You, Bull! Git up!"

They moved, creeping up the grade. A minute passed, two, three, four, five. The stage stopped. Bob Roberts opened the door.

"You can get out now," he said, almost gently.

The stage from Texas reached Gila City four hours late. Willing hands lifted out the dead guard. Dandy Bob Roberts, alighting, was seized upon by Old Man Duggan.

"You got my letter?" Duggan demanded. "It's a damn' good thing you come home."

"Letter? I never got a letter."

Dandy Bob pushed Duggan away. Gila City's deputy sheriff was at his elbow, requiring attention. "OK, Frank." With Deputy Frank McMain, the two drummers, and the stage driver, he shoved through the crowd to the livery stable's office.

In the office the details of the hold-up were recounted. Driver and traveling salesmen were profanely excited, while Dandy Bob was calm.

"We were just crawlin' on the Piegan Grade," the driver said. "There was a shot an' Mike went down. I stopped, an' he took another shot at the door, didn't he, Roberts?"

Dandy Bob nodded, and the driver continued his tale. "An' we never seen him. None of us seen him," he completed. "There wasn't no chance to make a fight. Mike had Roberts's gun an' them drummers didn't turn a hand. Just cold-blooded murder, that's what it was."

"He never yelled for us to stop. Just used his rifle," Bob corroborated. "An' I lost a bunch of clothes that Abe Meyer made for me. Cost me three hundred and fifty. I didn't like to lose that coat."

"He must be a new one," the deputy sheriff observed. "Ain't been anybody operatin' like that around here. Did you get your gun back, Bob?"

"As soon as I could," Bob assured. "Are you goin' out after him?"

McMain thought that over. "I reckon I'd better," he said ruefully. "It's late, too. You want to come?"

"I'm goin' home to bed," Bob answered. "You won't do any good. He's long gone."

McMain agreed. "But I guess I'd better go anyhow," he said. "The Butterfield people will have a man down here an' he'll want to know what I done. You'll be around, Bob, if I want you?"

"I'll be around," Bob agreed.

Old Man Duggan was waiting in the Rajah Saloon. Dandy Bob told the story of the stage hold-up to a group of eager listeners, took a drink, and, shaking off further questioners, forgathered with Duggan at a poker table in the rear of the room. For a wonder Old Man Duggan was almost sober, and he certainly was scared and glad to see Bob Roberts. The old man hardly waited for Bob to sit down before he began to tell his woes.

"I wrote you a letter," Duggan said. "I told you what happened. The widder caught on to me high-gradin' at the Limerick Girl. I told her it didn't make no difference . . . as long as we was goin' to get married, it was all in the fambly. But she didn't see it that away. She said we wasn't goin' to get married, an' she fired me."

Dandy Bob studied Duggan sardonically. He didn't give a damn about Old Man Duggan. Circumstances had thrown the two together and they shared a dubious fame. Once Dandy Bob and Old Man Duggan had delivered the Christmas mail to the mining camp of Freedom Hill, despite the obstacles raised by a band of Apaches. More recently they had, through no fault of their own, rediscovered the lost silver vein of the Widow Fennessy's Limerick Girl Mine. Six weeks ago, when Bob Roberts left for Tucson, Old Man Duggan had been sitting pretty, acting as minor boss at the Limerick Girl, drawing a hundred and fifty a month and high-grading at least that much more. And Duggan had been courting the grateful widow with all signs pointing to success.

"So you wrote me a letter?" Bob drawled. "I never got it. Hell! I didn't know you could write!"

Duggan disregarded the insult. "She's goin' to throw me in jail if I don't pay her back," he informed moodily.

Dandy Bob shrugged. "They say the jail's pretty comfortable. They make you work some, though. Maybe I'll get around to see you."

"You'll see me." Duggan's voice was grim. "You'll be right there with me. I know how you got your Tucson stake . . . don't forget that. I know about them cattle you rustled from the Seventy-Seven. If I go to jail, you'll be there, too, because I'll tell ol' Jim Conway who got his heifers. An' I can prove it! You're goin' to help me out, Bob. Don't think you ain't!"

Old Man Duggan. Liar, drunkard, no-account, good for nothing! If thoughts could kill, Old Man Duggan would have died in his chair.

"Well," said Dandy Bob Roberts. "Maybe I can help you, at that."

"Sure you can." Now that his blackmail had worked, Duggan brightened. "The widder likes you, Bob. You talk to her. Mebbe you can square me. This wouldn't've happened, anyhow, if it hadn't been for that damn' Max Fairfield."

"Fairfield! Who is he?"

"I wisht you'd got that letter," Duggan complained. "I wrote you about him. He come in here a week after you left an' bought the Bar Seven Cross. He stays in town mostly, an' he's been honeyin' up to the widder like a sick kitten to a hot rock. Over to her home every day an' night. Takin' her out to the Elite to eat an' down to the opery house when there's a show. He poisoned her ag'in' me, that's what he done. He wants to marry the Limerick Girl. He . . . that's him. Comin' in the door."

II

"NEW DUDE FOR GILA CITY"

Dandy Bob looked around. The man in the door of the Rajah was as tall and as broad-shouldered as Roberts himself. Moreover, his appearance mocked Bob's own. Dandy Bob Roberts had come by his name honestly. His were the finest clothes, the cleanest linen shirts, the most ornate trappings in Gila City, in Arizona Territory for that matter, and here was a man who put Dandy Bob to shame. Fairfield's coat was full and flared at the skirts, with a collar of black satin. His hat was broader than Dandy Bob's and blacker, too, if that was possible. His boots shone in the lamplight and, under his coat, disclosed as the garment swung, was a wide, carved belt of leather with a pearl-handled gun in the polished holster. Fairfield's eyes and hair were black as the hat, and a wisp of black mustache ornamented his lip.

Deliberately circling the crowd at the bar, Fairfield made his way toward the poker table, and Dandy Bob, aware of the dust upon him, automatically shrugged his coat square on his shoulders and brushed one sleeve. Envy filled Dandy Bob Roberts. If he just had the new coat Abe Meyers had made, he'd show this dude!

" 'Evenin', Duggan." Fairfield paused beside the table, opaque black eyes on Dandy Bob. "Missus Fennessy an' me have just been talkin' about you. Goin' to introduce your friend?"

Dandy Bob stood up. Duggan muttered what might have

been an introduction and Fairfield held out his hand. "Roberts, huh?" he said, and there was scorn in his tone. "Glad to meet you, Roberts. I heard about you. Have a drink?"

Dandy Bob had automatically taken the extended hand; now he let it go. There were two strikes on him and he knew it. So this—this walking clotheshorse—was the man who had undercut Old Man Duggan with the Widow Fennessy. An unwonted affection for that lying old drunkard mingled with antagonism toward Fairfield in Dandy Bob's mind.

"Not now," he drawled. "I just came in from Tucson. I think I'll go home an' clean up some."

"Stage trips sure get a man dirty," Fairfield commented. "I heard the stage got held up. Did you see who done it?"

"No." Dandy Bob shook his head. "Nobody saw him. Pleased to have met you, Mister Fairfield. Comin', Duggan?"

Outside the Rajah, Duggan spoke anxiously. "You're goin' to help me out, ain't you, Bob? You wouldn't go back on your pardner, would you? You ain't goin' to let no Fancy Dan like that get me throwed in the jug, are you? Why, Bob, that feller's got four or five suits of clothes, an' he changes his shirt every day!" There was a certain shrewdness in Old Man Duggan.

"So that's Fairfield, is it?" Dandy Bob glanced back toward the saloon. "That's the gent, huh? Yeah, I'll try to help you, Duggan. I'll go see the Widow Fennessy in the mornin'."

In the morning there was some debate about the visit to the widow. Duggan, who had spent the night with Bob, thought that he had better go along. Bob thought not, and carried his point. So, clean and refreshed, his clothing brushed and his boots polished, he left his solitary adobe at the edge of town, Duggan's directions still dinning in his ears.

The Widow Fennessy had changed her residence with the coming of prosperity. She no longer lived in a house on the Arroyo Seco, surrounded by clotheslines and flapping wash. Instead, the widow had purchased a small cottage near the center of Gila City. There were lace curtains at the windows and a bedraggled rosebush beside the door.

Bob knocked. Feet padded within the house and the door opened. Bob almost stepped back, he was so startled.

The Widow Fennessy had changed in six weeks. Here was a thing of art. Henna had restored and added to the beauty of the widow's red locks curled in a hundred ringlets about her broad face. Her cheeks were pink and white, and the carmine of her lips almost concealed the widow's small mustache. Her arms, which Bob remembered as red and muscled like a blacksmith's, were white now, although a freckle or two still showed through the powder, and her hands were soft as she seized Bob's.

"Bobby boy!" the widow exclaimed. "It's lovely of ye to come to see your Violet. An' just as soon as ye could, too. Come in! Come in!"

Dazed, Bob allowed himself to be led into the house. There was a rose-spattered Brussels carpet on the floor; the chairs and sofa were red plush; there were ornate gilt-framed pictures on the wall, and over all was an overpowering scent of heliotrope perfume.

"Sit down, Bobby. Sit down, do," the widow urged, and her voice was more dulcet than Daisy Mae's in Tucson had ever been. "An' tell me now, did ye enjoy yer trip?"

Bob sat down. Recovering, he looked about him. One of the pictures was a portrait view of Max Fairfield. There was work cut out for him, Bob saw. "Tucson's all right," he said. "Anyway. I left it that way. You're fixed things up, Missus Fennessy."

"You like it?" The widow smiled her pleasure. "It's not so much. Just a few things of me own. I've taste, Max says. You've met Max, Bobby boy?"

"Mister Fairfield?" Bob looked at the picture again. "Yeah, I met him. Missus Fennessy, I come over to see you. . . ."

"Missus Fennessy?" There was displeasure in the widow's tone. "Shure, me friends call me Violet." She rolled a coy eye at Dandy Bob. " 'Tis me name."

"Well, then, Violet,"—Dandy Bob choked a little—"I came over to see you about Duggan."

"Duggan, is it?" The widow's lips firmed and traces of the washwoman reappeared. "That scut'. That dirty, low-down . . . whist, now! I must remember I'm a lady. An' what about th' lyin' old thief, Bobby?"

Bob squirmed uncomfortably. "Well," he said, "I kind of talked to Duggan an' it seems like he got fired."

"An' for why?" the widow flared. "For stealin', that's why!" Anger cooled and the widow became coy again. "An' it was only because of you that he's not in jail entirely. You know how a girl is, Bobby. She has a weak spot for a handsome man."

Dandy Bob did not care for developments. There was a warmth in the widow's voice and a look in her eye that foretold trouble, and not for Old Man Duggan.

"Suppose Duggan was to pay back what he took?" Bob asked. "How much was it, anyhow?"

"About three hundred dollars, as near as I can figure out." Again the woman of economics showed in Mrs. Fennessy's face. "Of course, if he was to pay it back, an' you was to ask me, I'd forgive him." Again the roll of blue eyes.

"Well," Bob said, rising, "I'll see that he pays you back, Missus Fenn . . . Violet. I hope you won't have him arrested."

The widow had risen, too. She put her hands possessively on Bob's arm. "Of course I won't, now that you've asked me," she simpered. "An' you'll be comin' around to see Violet, won't you, Bobby? Max comes almost every day . . . but, of course, a girl with wealth an' looks doesn't want to tie herself down to one man."

Dandy Bob choked down swift words and forced a smile. "Sure, I'll be comin' around to see you," he agreed. "I got to see Duggan now an' fix it up so he'll pay you. Good bye . . . Violet."

"Good bye, Bobby." The widow, her hands still on Bob's arm, accompanied him to the door. "An' don't forget now . . . ye'll come to see me. Maybe we can have supper together at the Elite."

"Sure," agreed Dandy Bob and, wrenching open the door, escaped.

For two days following his visit to the widow, Dandy Bob Roberts stayed in Gila City. He had reported on his visit to an apprehensive and anxious Duggan, waiting for him at the adobe. Duggan was pleased that the widow did not intend to have him arrested immediately, but he was not otherwise satisfied. The old man had pinned his faith on Dandy Bob and it seemed that while Bob had not failed entirely, neither had he accomplished a complete success.

"You'd ought to've crowded her," Duggan chided. "Shucks! Didn't you go an' find the vein in the Limerick Girl for her? Don't she owe you somethin'? You'd ought to've made her come acrost."

"You're the one that's goin' to come across," Bob answered. "You're goin' to come across with three hundred bucks, that's what you're goin' to do."

The partners wrangled, both over Bob's visit and the

matter of payment. Neither had any amount of money nor did any appear in the immediate prospect. Bob played a little unfortunate poker, trying for a stake. Duggan pressed his credit at the Rajah and got drunk. And in the two days both saw Max Fairfield and the Widow Fennessy on the streets of Gila City. For Dandy Bob the widow had a smile and a pleasant word. Bob had promised to come to see her, she reminded. For Duggan she had a frown, and that was all.

Each time Bob and Duggan saw Fairfield, anger roused in them. Fairfield's wardrobe was a constant reminder to Bob of what might have been, save for the stage robbery. And Fairfield's contemptuous glances at Bob's year-old finery did nothing to assuage Bob's feelings. Nor did the comments of various acquaintances help. The bartender at the Rajah, the editor of the paper, even Watson, the assayer, remembering days when Bob's raiment shone in the sun and far surpassed their own, were not above making small, barbed comments.

As for Duggan, that old man hated Fairfield with a consuming passion. Except for Fairfield, Duggan believed, he would have been enjoying the warmth of the widow's parlor, drinking the widow's whiskey, living on the widow's credit, and basking in her charm. According to Old Man Duggan, Max Fairfield's coat concealed a barbed tail, his hat covered horns, and his polished boots hid cloven hoofs.

On the evening of the second day, Duggan came up with an idea. The widow had favored him with a particularly meaningful stare that afternoon and Duggan was worried.

"Look-it here, Bob," the old man suggested, "why don't you beat Fairfield's time with the widder? You could do it easy. She likes you, an' anyhow she owes you somethin' for findin' that vein in the Limerick Girl. Why don't you go down there an' cut Fairfield out?"

Bob frowned at Duggan. The last thing, the very last

thing, he wanted to do was beat anybody's time with the Widow Fennessy.

"You could even marry her," Duggan continued, musing. "Then we'd both be settin' pretty."

"Marry the widow?" Bob demanded.

"What's wrong with that? It beats goin' to jail. An' she wants to get married."

Duggan's last statement was true, as Dandy Bob well knew. And remembering the coy looks, the rolling eyes, and the soft hands of Violet Fennessy, he had no doubt but that Duggan was right on the other score, too. The widow had marriage in mind, all right, and—Bob shuddered slightly— she had Dandy Bob in mind, as well.

"What we got to do," he said, "is go out an' rustle three hundred dollars. Then nobody will have to marry the widow an' you won't go to jail."

"*We* won't go to jail," Duggan corrected. "How are we goin' to get the money? Hell, Bob, I wouldn't mind marryin' the widder. I'd *like* to."

"Then do it!" Dandy Bob snapped. "Save her life, or somethin', an' marry her. An' while you're waitin', see if you can't get the money. You ought to do it anyhow. Just to get even with Max Fairfield."

Bob did not explain how paying the widow would serve to spite Max Fairfield, but Duggan seemed to find merit in the suggestion. "*Ummm,*" he mused. "That's right, ain't it? I'll study on that, Bob."

"An' I'll see if I can't get the money," Bob promised.

The next morning, the third since his return, Bob roused early and, dressing without wakening Duggan, ate breakfast, and slipped out of his adobe. Since returning from Tucson he had retrieved his horse from the Star Livery and now, saddling the animal, he rode north from town.

There was a place where Bob knew he could get three hundred dollars with which to pay off Violet. There was a bank in the Huaraches, a never-failing checking account for Dandy Bob Roberts. It was dangerous to draw on the account, it was a hazardous undertaking, but Dandy Bob had made up his mind. Jim Conway's 77 ranch sprawled out over the Huaraches and the country about those hills. There were hidden cañons in the mountains. There were places where a brush corral could be built. Indeed, Bob knew where one was already built, for he had made it. Only—and here was the catch—Jim Conway was a fierce old devil who hired tough men. There was a constant patrol over the 77, and Jim Conway had a bad habit: he hung cow thieves.

Beyond Gila City, crossing the Arroyo Seco, Dandy Bob encountered a few cattle. These carried the Bar T Cross of Max Fairfield and Bob regretfully passed them by. The country was too open for rustling, too close to town. A man moving a bunch of Bar T Crosses would surely be caught. For eight miles he was on the Bar T Cross and then, entering the hills, was on range used by both Bar T and 77.

Staying below the skyline, using his knowledge of the country, alert and watchful, Bob rode on. And now he again saw cattle, big 77 steers, blocky 77 cows and heifers. Presently he entered a maze of cañons and rough country and, riding through piñons, cedar, and scrub oak, came to a little hidden cañon. The end of the cañon was blocked with brush and the walls rose sheer and straight. Dandy Bob Roberts grunted his satisfaction. The cañon was just as he had left it two months and more ago when he had stolen some 77 heifers for his Tucson grubstake.

III

"RUSTLERS' JAMBOREE"

Dismounting, he made a few minor repairs to the brush fence. Then, riding on, he climbed a ridge and, where aspens beset a little draw, stopped once more. While his horse grazed, he made a camp. Unrolling the slicker-wrapped blanket behind his saddle, he took out food and a battered can. That night Dandy Bob slept well despite the October chill, an aspen log smoldering on one side of him, a big rock reflecting heat back to warm the other side, his belly filled with coffee, cold biscuits, and beans, his nerves soothed by tobacco.

In the morning he was up betimes and at work. He cut out small bunches of cattle, making his selections carefully, and drove them to the hidden cañon. He had planned to take just enough to pay Duggan's debt to the widow, but the fever of the rustler took hold and possessed him. By mid-afternoon he had thirty head of 77 steers behind the brush fence.

Now he desisted from his labors. His horse, although grain-fed, would stand just so much work. The animal must rest. But when the moon rose at midnight, Dandy Bob planned to be right behind those steers, pounding them on the tail, driving them to Junction and a cow buyer he knew who would not ask embarrassing questions concerning ownership.

Bob closed the gap in the brush fence, waved a hand at the steers, and rode back to the aspen-choked draw. There he unsaddled and let his bay horse work on grama grass that was stirrup high, while he leaned back against the big rock, smoked a cigarette, and presently dozed off.

While Dandy Bob dozed, men were astir in the Huaraches and on the flats below the hills. Max Fairfield, riding a long circle, entered the maze of cañons and, striking a dim trail, followed it. The Widow Fennessy was on Fairfield's mind. He had come into the Gila City country and bought the Bar T Cross with one object in view: to steal cattle from his neighbors. In Gila City he had found the widow, apparently ripe and ready for plucking. But the widow was no bargain. She was shrewd for all her foolishness, and she had asked him how he could spend so much time in town when he had cattle to look after. Once before the widow had asked embarrassing questions.

Fairfield had staved her off then. Now he was in the hills, letting the widow grow lonely for his presence. He would spend a day or two at the ranch, he thought, and show her that he did have business in mind. Then, when he returned to Gila City, she would welcome him. He grinned as he thought about the widow and then, topping a rise, stopped his horse. A brush fence, blocking the end of a little box cañon, lay below him.

Cautiously, having wasted minutes scanning the country about, Fairfield rode on down. The cattle behind the fence wore the 77. Fairfield's grin broadened. He was an opportunist, and, if ever opportunity had come to his hand, this was the time. Thirty steers. Fairfield licked his lips. Then, turning his horse, he rode away. Behind a ridge in a little cove, he stopped and dismounted. His horse grazed on the good grama and Max Fairfield relaxed against a fallen log. Like Dandy Bob Roberts, he was waiting for the moon to rise.

Still another rider saw the steers behind the brush fence. Curley, a good, willing boy who worked for old Jim Conway, had spotted the brush corral a month before and reported its presence. Jim Conway had snorted when he heard the report.

"Don't drag down the fence," he ordered. "Keep an eye on it. Somebody used it once an' got away. They'll use it again, an', when they do, we'll get 'em."

Curley, riding out of a lonely line shack, kept daily check on the brush corral. He was returning to camp now as evening came, and he swung his ride so that the box cañon came under his observation. There were cattle behind the brush fence. Curley could see them. No need for closer inspection. They could be nothing but 77s. Curley turned his tired horse and struck out for headquarters, twenty miles away.

Half an hour after Curley had departed, there were sounds in the long draw leading to the brush fence. Cattle bellowed and a voice was raised in curses. Then, below the fence, cattle debouched into the open. Steers and cows these were, and on the right hip of each was a Bar T Cross. Presently the driver of the animals appeared. Old Man Duggan, tired by his unfamiliar occupation, sweating and with gray beard blowing in the wind, pulled to a stop, and stared incredulously. There were already cattle in the box cañon! Old Man Duggan swore.

For the first half day of Dandy Bob's absence, Old Man Duggan had moped around Gila City. In the afternoon he had encountered the widow. Pushing his luck, Duggan had spoken to that lady and the widow had blasted him. When, she demanded, was Duggan going to pay her? If not soon, then Duggan would go to jail. Thoroughly frightened, the old man had sought sanctuary in Dandy Bob's adobe and there, stimulated by whiskey, a plan had been born. Dandy Bob made money rustling cattle. Why not Aloysius Duggan? And whose cattle had better be stolen than those belonging to

Max Fairfield, Duggan's hated rival?

To think was to act. The bartender at the Rajah had staked Duggan to a pint. The bartender at the Mint had cautiously granted another. The barn boss at the Star Livery where Duggan once worked as hostler had, after much persuasion, consented to lend the old man a horse and saddle. Duggan went back to Dandy Bob's and drank one pint. In the morning, armed with the second bottle, he rode forth from Gila City on the livery stable nag. All day, undeterred by the objections that had stopped Bob Roberts, Old Man Duggan boldly put Bar T Cross cattle into a bunch and moved them toward the Huaraches. He knew the location of the hidden cañon and planned to halt there overnight. Now, having reached his destination, he found his haven occupied.

Old Man Duggan swore again. His labors could not be set aside so easily. He opened a gap in the brush and, entering the cañon, pushed out the 77s. Then, with the contented feeling that comes from a good deed well accomplished, he drove the Bar T Cross cattle through the opening, closed it, and, repairing to a site among some pines and two hundred yards from the fence, tied his horse and killed the remnants of the second pint. . . .

The moon came up, low and silver, with a nick out of its lower edge. Dandy Bob Roberts saddled his horse and wove a way through the aspens. He had a piece to go before daylight. He wanted to be far away when morning came. When he reached the brush fence, the moonlight was just beginning to enter the cañon. Bob dismounted, tied his horse, and approached the fence. As he reached it, he heard hoofs *clatter* on rock. He crouched in the shadow of the fence, hand on his gun, waiting. A rider came out through the trees. As the rider came nearer, Dandy Bob could see that he had been joined by Max Fairfield.

Fairfield stopped when he saw Bob's horse. His hand also rested on his gun butt. For an instant neither man moved. Then Fairfield said: "Who's there?"

Dandy Bob remained in the shadow, debating with himself. The sound of a shot carries a long way through a still night, but that fact did not deter Roberts. He waited because he was a gambler. A gambler takes chances, a gambler plays a square game.

"Who's there?" Fairfield repeated.

"None of your business!" Dandy Bob rasped. "Turn that horse around an' pull out of here. Keep goin'."

"Roberts!" Fairfield did not obey the command. Instead, he bent in his saddle, trying to pierce the gloom by the brush fence.

Dandy Bob wished now that he had drawn and fired. Fairfield knew him and there was no chance to get away unrecognized.

Fairfield laughed. "So you put 'em in there?" he said. "I wondered who done it. You'll have to count me in on this, Roberts."

Dandy Bob stepped out into the moonlight for concealment was no longer worthwhile. His hand was still on his gun and his voice was ominously calm. "How do you figure that?" he demanded.

"Because"—Fairfield's grin was wide—"Old Jim Conway hangs cow thieves, that's why."

"An' what's to stop me from leavin' you here for him to find?" Bob drawled. "Tell me that, Fairfield."

Apparently the idea had not occurred to Fairfield. He stared at Dandy Bob. "Why . . . ," he began, and hesitated.

In the silence the *clink* of metal against rock sounded, loud as a gunshot.

"Listen!" Fairfield exclaimed.

Again, and from a new direction, came the small sound of a horseshoe striking rock. Dandy Bob shrugged and dropped his hand from his gun butt. "How many have you got with you, anyhow?" he demanded.

Fairfield's face told him that his guess was wrong. Fairfield showed his sudden panic. He reined his horse around, facing toward the pine across the draw. The man was ready to run. There was movement against the dark loom of the pines.

A voice called: "Stay right where you're at! There's plenty of light to shoot by."

Bob Roberts knew that harsh rasp. It belonged to old Jim Conway. He glanced toward his horse. Maybe he could make it. Probably not. A showdown always comes sometime, and, when it comes, a man might as well face it. Bob Roberts thrust his hands into his pants pockets and waited. Five men rode out into the draw, coming from all angles, converging on the brush fence.

"Looks like you're caught this time." Conway rasped. "I been layin' for you, Roberts."

The riders halted as Conway spoke again. "An' Fairfield, too. I been wonderin' why you bought that little wad of Bar T Crosses. Now I know."

Panic filled Fairfield's voice. "They're not my cattle, Mister Conway. I got nothin' to do with 'em. Roberts put 'em in there. They're not mine."

Five guns, three of them rifles, covered the two men by the fence. Jim Conway seemed to find the situation amusing. "So they ain't yours, huh?" he demanded. "You got nothin' to do with 'em. That right?"

"Not a thing." Fairfield thought that Conway was going to let him go. "Roberts put 'em there."

One of the 77 riders moved, passing Dandy Bob, pausing at the fence. Conway, still playful, rasped: "Is that right, Roberts?"

Dandy Bob shrugged. "You heard the man," he answered.

"Hey, Mister Conway!" The rider at the fence sounded worried. "There's somethin' wrong here. I just seen a brand. It ain't no 77."

Dandy Bob's heart leaped up and filled his throat. His head reeled. Not a 77? It couldn't be! He had put those cattle in the pen himself. He knew the brands.

"What?" Jim Conway roared.

"It ain't no 77 on this one. Looks like a Bar T Cross."

"Curley!" If ever a man was angry, it was Jim Conway. "I thought you said you'd seen these cattle. I thought you said they were mine!"

Curley's voice was apologetic. "I didn't think to ride down to look at 'em, Mister Conway. I seen 'em from up above an' I thought they belonged to us. I didn't want to. . . ."

Jim Conway's order interrupted Curley. "Git down, all of you. Bill, take the guns off them two jaspers. Henry, you an' Mike git inside an' build a fire. We're goin' to look at them cattle. There's somethin' around here that stinks."

Dandy Bob relaxed. He even grinned thinly at the men who removed his gun. Something had happened here that Dandy Bob did not understand, but he knew it had happened. Jim Conway, feet widespread, stood between Dandy Bob and Max Fairfield, staring first at one, then the other. Behind the brush fence a man struck a match and a feeble flame flickered, adding to the moonlight. Dry brush was tossed on and the fire roared up.

"Look at *all* them cattle!" Conway shouted. "Every damn' one of 'em."

"This here's Bar T Cross," a rider answered.

"So is this'n."

93

Dandy Bob looked at Max Fairfield. Incredulity, anger, and a dawning realization mingled on Fairfield's face. Suddenly Dandy Bob grinned. How 77 steers had been changed to Bar T Cross cattle Bob did not know, but he did realize—and the knowledge struck him with the force of a blow—that Max Fairfield had disclaimed the cattle behind the fence. Fairfield had said they were not his own, that they belonged to Dandy Bob Roberts. And Fairfield owned the Bar T Cross!

Behind the brush fence work progressed rapidly. It doesn't take long, even by moon and firelight, to examine the brands on some thirty head of animals, particularly when those animals are bunched and the brands are plain. The fire died down and Conway's men came from the pen.

"They're all Bar T Crosses," one reported.

For a moment no one spoke. Then Conway wheeled to Fairfield. "An' you said they were Roberts's cattle!" he accused.

Max Fairfield was caught on the horns of a dilemma. He had disclaimed ownership of the cattle behind the fence and he couldn't change his statement. How could he tell Jim Conway that he had believed the penned animals to be 77s? Any such statement was practically a confession of theft. He had said that the cattle belonged to Dandy Bob and he was stuck with the statement.

"That's what I said," he admitted reluctantly.

Jim Conway wheeled on Dandy Bob. "What are you doin' with cattle on my range?" he demanded. "You know I won't stand for that. I'll give a man a pilot across my country, but I want to know who's movin' what. You'd better talk up, Roberts."

Dandy Bob shrugged by way of answer. Conway's wrath increased. There was something here he did not understand, and anything Jim Conway did not understand was wrong.

"Where were you takin' 'em?" he demanded. "I suppose you just come along an' decided to pen 'em up overnight, an' then, when the moon came up, you thought you'd move along again?" There was heavy sarcasm in the ranchman's voice.

"Somethin' like that," Dandy Bob admitted.

"Yeah . . . somethin' like that! If Fairfield here hadn't said they was your cows, I'd think you'd stole 'em, but he ought to know. Where were you plannin' to take 'em?"

"To Junction." Dandy Bob thought he might as well tell the truth.

"An' across my country, too. You know I don't like that, Roberts."

"I didn't want to bother you," Dandy Bob answered. He was still telling the truth. "There's just a little bunch of 'em."

Conway appeared to be somewhat mollified. "I don't mind bein' bothered," he rasped.

An idea struck Dandy Bob. "I meant to sell 'em," he said. "Would you be interested, Mister Conway?"

Jim Conway was always interested in cattle, particularly when they were cheap. "Depends on the price," he said.

"We could look 'em over," Bob suggested. "I don't think I'd be too high. I got 'em cheap enough." It was a pleasure to see Fairfield squirm.

Conway looked at Dandy Bob, then at Fairfield. "Suppose I bought 'em," he asked. "There wouldn't be no kickbacks?"

Dandy Bob waited for Fairfield to answer. "No kickbacks," Fairfield choked.

"I got to look 'em over by daylight," Conway warned. "An' I didn't say I'd buy 'em."

"I don't mind waitin'." Dandy Bob's voice was smooth. "If you buy 'em, it saves me a drive." He was determined now that Conway should have the cattle. Nobody, Max Fairfield or anyone else, would take those cows away from Jim Conway once he had paid for them. "It'll be sunup after a while."

"Well . . . ," Conway said dubiously.

Dandy Bob Roberts spoke politely to Max Fairfield. "There ain't no need of you stayin'," he said.

"I want my gun back," Fairfield announced sullenly.

"Give him his gun," Conway directed. "Give 'em both back their guns."

Jim Conway was enjoying the situation now. He knew that there was something amiss between Roberts and Fairfield. He didn't know what it was, but Roberts was putting over something. Conway sensed it. Fairfield had said that the cattle belonged to Dandy Bob and in the presence of witnesses. Dandy Bob was offering to sell the cattle. Jim Conway scented a bargain. And, too, in old Jim Conway, there was a sneaking fondness for Bob Roberts.

"I guess Roberts is right, Fairfield," old Jim Conway said. "Likely him an' me'll trade. There's no use of your stayin'."

Max Fairfield stuffed his restored weapon into its holster. He looked up at the moon, bright overhead. "I'll go to the ranch."

Curley, relegated to the job of horse holder, extended a pair of reins. Fairfield took them, mounted, and, without looking back, rode off.

"Somethin' stuck in his craw," Jim Conway said, watching Fairfield disappear.

"Likely he figures he let me have these cattle too cheap," drawled Dandy Bob. "Say, don't that sound like another horse movin'?"

Conway listened. "I don't hear it," he said. "What do you want for them cattle, Roberts?"

Dandy Bob was still listening and did not answer immediately. Dandy Bob was right. There were two horses moving, and the second horse was Old Man Duggan's.

IV

"HUSBAND FOR THE WIDOW?"

Just after dinner Dandy Bob Roberts rode warily into Gila City. After some haggling, he had sold the Bar T Cross cattle to Jim Conway for twenty dollars a head. Conway's check for six hundred dollars was in Bob's pocket, and he kept his hand close to it.

When he reached his adobe, Old Man Duggan came out to meet him. Duggan's face looked like a storm over the mountains.

"Stole 'em, that's what you done!" Duggan accused. "You stole my cows!"

"Now, wait!" Bob held up a detaining hand. "What's the matter with you? Stole your cows? You never had no cows!"

"The hell I didn't!" Duggan preceded Bob into the single room of the house, talking over his shoulder. "I worked like hell all day yesterday gettin' them cows together. I drove 'em into that pen. I was goin' to rest a while an' then take 'em on."

Dandy Bob Roberts sat down on his bed and stared weakly at his accuser. The mystery of the Bar T Cross cattle was explained. It had been Duggan who put them into the pen, substituting them for the steers Bob had so carefully selected.

"*You* rustled them Bar T Crosses?"

"You're damn' right it was me!"

Dandy Bob fell back on the bed and howled with laughter.

"It ain't so damn' funny," Old Man Duggan declared defensively. "I worked hard for them cows."

"An' Fairfield said I owned 'em. An' I sold 'em to Conway. This'll kill me yet!" Bob managed to get the words out through his merriment. "Lord, Duggan! What'll you do next?"

"I'll collect from you, that's what I'll do," Duggan stated wrathfully.

"I wish you'd seen Fairfield's face," Dandy Bob gasped. "Conway come ridin' down, all fixed for war, an' Fairfield couldn't wait to tell him them cattle was mine an' that he didn't have a thing to do with 'em."

"I heard it." Some of Duggan's anger departed. "I was layin' over in the trees, an' I heard the whole thing. I pulled out when Fairfield left."

After a time the two sobered sufficiently for Bob to tell Duggan the aftermath, of how he had sold the Bar T Cross cattle.

"I stayed a while to watch him vent brands," Bob informed. "I got his check for six hundred in my pocket."

"Half of it's mine," Duggan claimed.

Bob made no denial. "Enough to pay off Widow Fennessy," he agreed. "Let's go cash the check. Then we'll go see her an' square up. An' we got to look out for Fairfield. He's plenty mad an' he'll maybe start somethin'."

"I'd like to see him try!" Duggan got up and, walking to the door, picked up a shotgun from the rack beside it.

They delayed only long enough for Bob to unsaddle and feed his horse. When that was taken care of, the two headed for town, Bob walking in the lead, old Duggan trailing.

In Gila City's small bank the check was cashed and, filled with high good spirits, the two went on toward the Widow Fennessy's. They were not ten yards from the cottage when Frank McMain hailed them.

"Hey, Roberts!"

Bob turned. The deputy sheriff, accompanied by another man, was hurrying down the street. The two drew up.

"This here is Lon Bowers," McMain announced. "He's workin' for the Butterfield Stage Line. They sent him in here about that robbery."

Dandy Bob and Duggan shook hands with the Butterfield man. Bowers was square-built and stocky, with competence written large upon him. "I want to talk to you about that hold-up," he announced.

"I can't tell you much," Bob answered good-naturedly. "I didn't see much. That hold-up was cagey."

"I'd like to ask you some questions just the same," Bowers said. "If you got time."

"I got the time." Bob grinned. "Me an' Duggan got a little business an' then I'll be loose. I'll meet you downtown an' answer any questions I can. I'd like to get that coat back. It was. . . ."

Dandy Bob stopped. His eyes widened as he stared past McMain and Bowers. The Widow Fennessy, accompanied by Max Fairfield, had come from the cottage. The widow turned to lock the door, and Fairfield, glancing up the street, scowled at Dandy Bob and the men with him. But it was not the scowl that checked Bob's speech, rather it was the coat that Fairfield wore. There was no mistaking that coat. Shining satin collar, broad, square-padded shoulders, sweeping, bell-like tails, the coat shrieked out what it was: Abe Meyer's best handicraft. Bob Roberts's coat, stolen in the stage robbery.

"That's it!" Dandy Bob gasped. "That's my coat! Right there! Fairfield's got it on!"

"Are you sure?" Bowers's voice was low and harsh. "Are you plumb sure, Roberts?"

"Of course, I'm sure!" Dandy Bob had recovered from his

surprise. "Think I don't know it? I ordered them wide cuffs on the sleeves." He started to pass Bowers and was thrust back.

"That is my business!" Bowers snapped, and moved toward Max Fairfield. "Hey, you! I want to talk to you."

The widow had finished locking her door and turned as Bowers called. Fairfield, perhaps recognizing the Butterfield man, certainly aware that he was being called, stepped away from the widow. As he moved, he reached under the coat. His gun came out and he turned and ran.

"Halt!" McMain thundered. "Halt, or I'll shoot!" The deputy had his gun out. He raised it as Fairfield continued to run, and Dandy Bob pushed the deputy sheriff's arm. He couldn't take chances on that coat's being ruined. McMain's shot kicked up dust in the street. Dandy Bob leveled his own gun, aiming at Fairfield's legs.

Before Bob could pull trigger, Fairfield wheeled and fired twice, once at Dandy Bob, once at Bowers. The first shot missed, but Bowers flinched as he was hit.

Old Man Duggan fled, losing his courage and the shotgun at the same time. Being a target was no part of Duggan's business as he understood it. The Widow Fennessy was the biggest thing in sight, and Duggan, dropping, ran for shelter. The widow, as frightened as Duggan, saw him coming. There was more than two hundred pounds of the Widow Fennessy and about a hundred and forty pounds of Old Man Duggan. The widow received him in her ample arms.

Bob caught just a glimpse of this, of Duggan dangling, with his feet off the ground. Of the widow's frightened face, peering over Duggan's shoulder. He centered his attention on Fairfield once again, trying for a shot, but Bowers was in the way.

"Don't hit that coat!" Dandy Bob rasped.

Bowers was not bothered by consideration of clothing. He

had been hit once and Fairfield was leveling off to shoot again. The Butterfield man snapped two quick shots, one on the heels of the other, and Max Fairfield, surprise supplanting the hatred on his face, bowed forward, bending very slowly at the middle, and then pitched down on his face. Bowers, McMain, and Dandy Bob ran to the fallen man. McMain bent and, with an effort, turned Fairfield so that he lay upon his back.

"Plumb center," the deputy announced.

"You never touched it," said Dandy Bob, fingering the fine broadcloth. "Never touched the coat at all!"

At ten o'clock that night Dandy Bob Roberts sat at a poker table in the Rajah Saloon. Lamps in wall brackets and in the chandelier overhead shed their brilliance upon him; across the table were Frank McMain and Lon Bowers. Bowers, his shoulder bandaged and his voice tired, was talking.

"So we found the express box an' a lot of other stuff hid at the ranch. There was a sample case of jewelry an' a lot of clothes. Yours among 'em, I reckon. I guess that ranch hand out there don't know much about it. Leastwise, he says he don't, an' we got nothin' to hold him on. But it was Fairfield that held up the stage an' killed the guard."

"An' Fairfield's dead," said Dandy Bob.

"Yeah," Bowers agreed heavily. "He's dead. The stage company puts up a hundred dollars reward on hold-ups, Roberts. That'll be split between you an' McMain. I can't take reward money."

"You can give my part to the guard's folks," said Dandy Bob.

"Mine, too." McMain nodded agreement.

"Then that's all, I guess." Bowers got up stiffly. McMain, too, arose.

When they were gone, Dandy Bob lingered, fingering the roll of bills in his pocket. Duggan was at the Widow Fennessy's and Dandy Bob had promised to wait for Old Man Duggan. Fifteen minutes went past.

Duggan walked in with a swinging stride, high, wide, and handsome. He plunked himself down in a chair opposite Dandy Bob and stared loftily at his partner. Dandy Bob pulled out the roll of bills.

"I meant to give you your half before you went down there," he said apologetically. "Three hundred dollars."

"Three hundred dollars!" Duggan scoffed. "Chicken feed! You keep it. Me an' Vi'let are goin' to git married right away. What do I want with three hundred dollars? I got the Limerick Girl!"

"Yeah?" Dandy Bob returned the money to his pocket. "So you're getting married?"

"Right away. Vi'let's come to her senses. She says, when I run over there to her rescue, she knowed I was her own true love. She says young fellers are all right, but it takes a mature man like me to shield an' protect a woman."

"An' you're all fixed up now?" Dandy Bob tapped the felt table top with long, slender fingers.

"All fixed up." Duggan arose from the chair. "I just come down to tell you not to wait for me. I'm goin' back to Vi'let's a while. We're talkin' things over."

"That's fine." Dandy Bob smiled faintly. "I'll leave the door open so you can get in. Good night."

" 'Night, Bob." Old Man Duggan stalked away.

Dandy Bob continued to tap the tabletop. It had, he considered, been a good day. He had six hundred dollars, come by more or less honestly. He had helped to catch a murderer and stage robber. And he had—and this was the important item—recovered his clothes. Once they were cleaned and pressed they would grace his form and enhance his reputation as the best-dressed man in Gila City. He would, he decided, wear the coat to Old Man Duggan's wedding.

The Joke
in Hell's Backyard

I

"DANGER PRESCRIBED"

As social arbiter and patron of the arts it fell to Dandy Bob Roberts to quell the riot in the Gila City Opera House. The occasion was the appearance of Madame Simone Tetri, late of the Milan opera and recalled to the United States, so the handbill said, by popular demand. The time was the end of the month—pay day—and the hardy souls who delved for silver ore, or who choused cattle on the sun-baked ranges about town, were present in force. As later reported in the *Gila City Herald*: **There were many of the hoi-polloi mingled with the cognoscenti.**

Madame Tetri appeared in concert. Dandy Bob, befitting his position, occupied a box. His guests were the Widow Fennessy and Old Man Duggan who, so Duggan hoped, were shortly to be united in connubial bliss. The widow was corseted until her eyes bugged out; three layers of powder hid her freckles. Duggan, morosely unhappy in a starched shirt, sucked surreptitiously on a bottle in the rear of the box while the widow and Dandy Bob displayed their finery in front.

Below, among the common herd, perspiring bar girls sought to assuage month-old thirsts, hurrying from bar to customer with many a foaming flagon, many a thick-bottomed glass of whiskey. It was a gala scene, made more so by the arrival in the opposite box of *Don* Filiberto Paiz, *grandee* from Rancho Santisima. *Don* Filiberto was a power in Mexican politics and Duggan's friend. Dandy Bob was about to comment upon this unwonted occurrence when the curtain went up. Following a suitable pause, Madame Tetri rustled onto the stage. Immediately the widow envied madame her corsets, Duggan forgot his bottle, and a raucous soul in the pit shouted: "Sing 'Annie Laurie'!"

Madame bowed to the applause and plunged into the "Suicido!" aria from *La Gioconda*. Which has as many high spots as the Chiricahua Mountains. She was a coloratura soprano with a voice that could easily have supported the roof of the opera house.

At the conclusion of the number there was a spattering of applause, Duggan, who liked his women big, furnishing at least a third. The sentimental person in the pit, re-voiced his request: "Sing 'Annie Laurie'!" Dandy Bob, frowning portentously, leaned over the box railing and sought out the speaker. He did not identify the gentleman but he did spot Daffyd ap Griffiths, just in from the Dragoon Mountains and doubtless with money in his poke. Daffyd was a successful prospector and the last time he'd struck town Bob had won five hundred. He made a mental note of Daffyd.

Madame Tetri next sang a group of three German *Lieder,* soft and touchingly sentimental. They appealed to the crowd and Daffyd, Welchman and music lover, closed his eyes and swayed gently. The gentleman who wanted "Annie Laurie" again mentioned his desire in a somewhat thickened voice. There were hisses of protest from a portion of the audience, but he had backers who spoke loudly. The accompanist raked the piano keys and Madame Tetri began— *"Ah, fors' è lui che l'anima."*—loud and long and with plenty of fireworks. Dandy Bob thoughtfully felt of his gun butt, concealed under his broadcloth coat. Gila City's marshal was not present and through long experience Bob scented trouble.

At the conclusion of *"Ah, fors,"* the audience divided. A

few applauded, but "Annie Laurie" had her adherents. Daffyd ap Griffiths stood up and stared, stony-faced, at a large man behind him. Dandy Bob had also selected the large man as the "Annie Laurie" leader. Hisses and applause were equal in volume and someone in the back of the house demanded that madame dance. Dandy Bob thrust a long leg over the box railing and Daffyd hit the big man in the face.

Bill Fay, owner of the Opera House, and three bartenders now advanced from the rear. An enthusiast, probably the man who craved dancing, loosed a shot at the roof. Madame Tetri, all one hundred and ninety pounds of her, took refuge under the big, square piano. Old Man Duggan, drunk as usual, and never one to let a woman go undefended, joined her there, his left arm around the lady's iron-bound waist, a gun in his right hand, and his bewhiskered face thrust forward combatively. The large man, who was a stranger in Gila City, knocked Daffyd down, and Dandy Bob, arriving, placed his Colt with force and precision against the large man's head. The large man slept, Bill Fay and the bouncers arrived, the bar girls screamed, and Widow Fennessy gave a war whoop and started after Duggan.

With their leader down, the "Annie Laurie" partisans lacked unity. Dandy Bob jumped to the stage and, gun in hand, ordered the crowd to sit down, shouting that the concert would continue. Such was not to be. The widow hauled Duggan from beneath the piano, gripping him by one kicking leg. The curtain came down and Bill Fay, knowing the sure way to stop the commotion, shouted that the drinks were on the house. Two men were trampled in the rush that ensued. Dandy Bob found himself staring at heaving backs in place of belligerent faces and, recalling his financial status, hurdled benches and picked up the recumbent Daffyd.

Such was the concert at the Gila City Opera House. In reporting the event the *Herald* was apologetic, albeit a trifle stern.

> **Gila City has disgraced itself. Madame Tetri, the victim of the recent disgraceful scene, is recuperating from her nervous shock in the New York Hotel, under the care of our popular physician, Doc Speers.**

> **The *Herald* bewails the actions of certain of our inhabitants but, at the same time, can see the cause. Gila City has her likes and dislikes and she does not care for Italian opera. After all, "Annie Laurie" is a nice song.**

In its report the *Herald* failed to mention various important occurrences. Dandy Bob won no money from Daffyd ap Griffiths who, having recovered, departed the confines of a community so inartistic. The big stranger left town, his exodus unnoticed. *Don* Filiberto traveled on toward Tucson, where he had business of importance, and the Widow Fennessy called off her engagement to Old Man Duggan.

This last matter was forcibly brought to Dandy Bob's attention when, at noon next day, he took his pre-meal liquor. Old Man Duggan came moping into the Rajah Saloon and put fifty cents on the bar. It was so unusual for Duggan to buy a drink that Dandy Bob knew something was wrong.

"What's in your craw?" he asked Duggan. "You look lower'n the Limerick Girl shaft."

"The widdy," Duggan said, having tossed off his whiskey. "She ain't goin' to marry me."

"So? Why not?"

"On account of last night. I went under the pianner to help

that singin' woman an' the widdy claims I was makin' love to her."

Here was a problem. Circumstances had thrown Dandy Bob and Duggan together on several occasions and, while Bob had no particular love for the old man, he did feel a certain responsibility. Widow Fennessy owned the Limerick Girl Mine that, since Dandy Bob and Duggan had accidentally found the lost vein, was a source of wealth. Duggan had attached himself to Dandy Bob and, if the widow called off the wedding, two things would happen: a source of richness that Bob expected to tap would be closed to him, and he would have the responsibility for Duggan. Bob did not want to be forced to look after the lying old whelp.

"You'd ought to've stayed with the widow," he chided. "Why didn't you?"

"Well," Duggan admitted sheepishly, "I never seen no woman like that primmy donny. I wanted to see what she felt like."

"An' now the widow's mad," Dandy Bob said. "Jealous, likely."

"She's sore as hell," Duggan confirmed. "Says she never wants to see me no more. An' she fired me at the Limerick Girl, too."

This was the second time Duggan had been relieved of his job as shift boss of the Limerick Girl. The first time he had been fired for high-grading.

"You got to do somethin' about it, Bob," Duggan continued. "You got to get me in good again."

Dandy Bob swore. Why, he demanded, by all that was good should he concern himself with Duggan's troubles?

"You will," Duggan said. "Buy me a drink, Bob."

Duggan was possessed of certain knowledge, and Dandy Bob knew that the old man was right. Bob Roberts would help Duggan, or else. . . . He bought a drink. Indeed, he bought two drinks and in their consuming studied the problem. "Women," he said, when the second drink had gone the way of all good whiskey, "are sentimental. If you was to go away, Duggan . . . if you was to be in danger . . . the widow would come around."

"What kind of danger?" Duggan was practical.

"Apaches," Bob said. "Mebbe if the Apaches was to get you. . . ."

Duggan shuddered at the thought and Dandy Bob shook his head. "That won't do," he said. "They'd kill you. No loss, neither. Maybe if you was kidnapped, or somethin'. . . . I'll study on it, Duggan, an' you do the same."

They parted then, Dandy Bob for the Elite Restaurant, Duggan for the Star Livery barn where he had once worked as hostler.

Raphael Sena had taken Duggan's former job. Raphael was a bright, upstanding young man with sympathy for such persons as were down on their luck. It being noon, the livery barn was deserted and Raphael and Duggan forgathered in the feed room where Raphael had a bottle, Duggan drank and thought while Raphael sympathized.

Liquor aroused an inventive streak in the old man. Halfway down the quart an idea struck him. The seed, planted by Dandy Bob, budded and brought forth flowers.

"Look-it here, Raphael," Duggan said. "You can write, can't you?"

Raphael admitted the weakness. He had completed the fourth grade in the Sisters' School, he said.

"Then," Duggan announced, "I want you to write me a letter. I'm goin' to have the Sisneros boys kidnap me, I am. They're goin' to hold me for five thousand dollars ransom.

You write the letter to the Widow Fennessy."

Raphael brought paper and pencil from the barn office. Duggan worked on the quart and dictated. The result was a masterpiece. Raphael, at Duggan's instigation, demanded five thousand dollars for the return of Old Man Duggan. The note was addressed to Violet Fennessy, and warned that, should the money not be paid, the widow would receive Duggan's ears, one at a time.

"Now," Duggan ordered, "sign the Sisneros boys' names an' gimme it."

"The Sisneros?" Raphael looked up. "They want to keednap you?"

"Of course not," Duggan scoffed, "but they're the toughest outfit I can think of right now. Go on an' put their names down."

"But 'ow," Raphael persisted, "eef the Sisneros do not keednap you, weel you be keednap?"

"I'll get a friend to take me offen the stage."

"An' these Weedow Fennessy? She weel pay the money?"

"Sure." Duggan felt large and cheerful. "She'll pay. She don't think no more of me than she does of her right arm."

"An' eef the Sisneros keednap you, they weel get pay?"

"Yeah. *If* they kidnapped me. But they ain't goin' to. Go on an' put their names down an' gimme the note. An' you keep still about this, Raphael. You keep your mouth shut, hear me?"

Raphael signed two names and pasted the paper over. "Theese keednap ees profitable beesiness," he said wistfully.

"You're damn' right." Duggan gave Raphael a dollar and pocketed the note. "Now you keep shut, Raphael. So long." Bottle still in hand, he left the livery barn.

He went home, to Dandy Bob's solitary adobe at the edge of town. There he killed the bottle and, finding more whiskey on hand, saw that it, too, was not wasted. He thought as he drank and, when he finally passed out, was hazy but pleased concerning his whole plan. He would get Dandy Bob to stop the stage and take him off, and Dandy Bob could send the kidnap note. Then, after a suitable time, Duggan would return, boasting of his escape. Surely Violet would reward his bravery. When Dandy Bob came in, much later, Duggan was snoring.

Raphael, when Duggan left, went back to work. Ostensibly Raphael's business in life was to act as hostler, and he played the part. At six o'clock he left the site of his endeavors and, later that night, appeared in Pablo Ablano's *cantina* in Gila City's Mexican town. There he drank tequila with two swarthy, big-hatted men, and presently drifted out into the quiet night with them.

The three talked and smoked and, after a time, Raphael's companions left, riding south on chunky Mexican ponies, their big-roweled spurs *jingling*. Raphael went back to Pablo's and had another drink, well pleased with himself. As hostler at the Star he was able to keep an eye on things, to note valuable shipments out of Gila City, to hear gossip and glean the news. Raphael was a spy for the Sisneros brothers, a most valuable member of the gang, and this evening he had conducted a particularly good bit of business. The men he talked with were Luz and Chacon Sisneros themselves, and, when Old Man Duggan was kidnapped from the westbound stage, there would be no fake about it. The Widow Fennessy was going to pay $5,000 to the Sisneros. If she didn't, she would receive Duggan's ears, one at a time. Luz had said he would preserve the ears in salt.

II

"A JOB AT BRONCHO HOUSE"

Dandy Bob Roberts, returning to his accustomed seat in the Rajah, found that he had company. Three men were seated around the poker table, the bartender hovered obsequiously, and there were clean glasses and a quart bottle of Chapin & Gore on the green felt. Bob shook hands. His visitors were not run-of-the-mill in any sense. They were from Tucson and occupied places of prominence in that town. Gene Bertram, Tucson's city marshal, Gus Hoehn, and Harvey Louthian, merchants of the Old Pueblo, each greeted Dandy Bob, and Bertram invited him to sit down.

"We've been waitin' for you," Bertram announced. "We came down on the stage an' we're goin' back tonight. Have a drink, Bob."

It was too soon after dinner for a drink, Dandy Bob said as he took a seat. It was not often he was privileged to sit in with the mighty and his curiosity was aroused.

"Doin' anything in particular right now?" Bertram asked.

"Nothin' special," Bob answered.

"We've got," said Bertram, "a little somethin' on our minds. There's pretty good money in it an' we thought we could interest you."

"Spit it out, Gene," Hoehn ordered. "Don't beat around the bush. We've got a job for you, Bob. We want you to take over Broncho House."

Broncho House, thirty miles from Gila City, was a deserted ranch at the end of the Dragoons and close to the border. There were tales concerning the place; strange things were said to happen there. Dandy Bob leaned forward.

"Gus an' Harvey an' me are doin' a little tradin' these days," Bertram said. "We're tradin' goods for 'dobe dollars."

Dandy Bob sat back again. He knew now what this was all about. Smuggling along the border was a well-organized, almost recognized business. No one looked down on a smuggler. To take calico and iron pots, weapons and ammunition, the various products of the United States, and trade them for big, silver *pesos* was both lucrative and acceptable. Why pay import duty to the government of Porforio Días when the border was long and the nights were dark?

"Yeah?" Bob said.

"That's right." Bertram nodded agreement. "We've been sellin' in Mexico for some time an' we need a man."

"Haven't you got one?" Bob asked.

"We've had Soldier Deutch down there," Bertram answered. "Know him?"

"I've never met him," Bob said.

It was true. He had not met Soldier Deutch, in the flesh, but he knew his reputation. Deutch was a very hardcase in a country where the average man had to be hard in order to exist. Deutch had received his name due to trouble in El Paso where he had tangled with a half squad of buffalo soldiers. When the smoke died, Deutch was riding southwest and the half squad had been excessively reduced.

"We've been doin' business with the Sisneros boys on the other side," Bertram continued.

Here again were men that Bob Roberts had never seen but of whose reputation he was aware. Luz and Chacon Sisneros were rising in the public eye. Beginning as simple *peones,* they had successfully raided two ranches below the line, acquiring wealth, horses, and followers. From that beginning they had branched out, being enterprising. The word was that the last two stage hold-ups had been conducted by the Sisneros and their followers.

"Kind of tough, ain't they?" Bob suggested.

"You've got to do business with tough people in this trade," Bertram answered. "We didn't want to take in the Sisneros boys but we had to. If we hadn't, they'd've declared themselves in anyhow."

To that statement Bob nodded agreement. The Sisneros boys had perhaps thirty followers. Both goods and 'dobe dollars required transportation, and, while the average Mexican smuggler was no dove of peace, still, he wouldn't stack up too high against the bloodthirsty Sisneros or they would take over.

"What we want," Bertram continued, "is a man down there we can trust. We want somebody who ain't afraid to burn a little powder an' who is honest. An' we been hearin' things about you. We know how you downed Tom Harmes, an' run Press Bell an' Shorty Winn out of the country. We heard how you gave the Limerick Girl back to Missus Fennessy when you had an option on it. We know about you tanglin' with the Apaches when you took the mail through to Freedom Hill last Christmas. We figure you ain't afraid an' that you're honest."

The fruits of unearned reputation were coming home. On each of the occasions mentioned, Dandy Bob Roberts had been forced to react honestly when utterly dishonest motives had put him in a precarious position.

"Uhn-huh," he said. "What's in this business for me?"

"Money," Louthian said bluntly. "Plenty of money. We think Soldier is knockin' down on us, an' yet we made ten thousand last month. We'll pay you five hundred a month."

Dandy Bob smiled faintly and shook his head. "I want a fourth," he said. "One fourth of the profits."

"A fourth?" Hoehn almost squalled, subsiding as the others hissed for silence. "A fourth?" he said more quietly. "That's twenty-five hundred dollars! That's. . . ."

"Your man Soldier is gettin' more than that," Bob interrupted, "or else you wouldn't be here. Look, gentlemen. You want me to go down an' take over from Soldier Deutch. Soldier is on the shoot and you know it. He ain't goin' peaceful. You want me to work with the Sisneros brothers, an' they'd rather cut your throat than look at you. It's one fourth or nothin' with me. That's my word."

Bertram looked at his companions. Hoehn's head tipped slightly and Louthian also nodded. Gene Bertram was no peaceful citizen; he had come to be Tucson's city marshal the hard way, through smoke.

"Why don't you go yourself, Gene?" Dandy Bob asked.

"Because I can't afford to be out of Tucson right now," Bertram answered. "All right. We'll make it a fourth. Let's take a drink on it." He reached for the bottle of Chapin & Gore.

For a while longer the four men drank and talked. Bob was instructed in certain ramifications of the smuggling business. Plans were also made. He would, Bob said, go down to Broncho House and look over the situation. Then, when he knew how many men he needed to take over the job, return to Gila City and hire them.

They took a final drink. "We've just about got time to get the stage north," Bertram announced. "We're leavin' it with you, Roberts. As soon as we hear, we'll start five or six wagonloads to you. An' "—he paused for an instant—"I hope we ain't been wrong in pickin' you for the job. If we have, it's going to be too bad . . . for you. So long."

The Tucson gentry left. Bob, surveying the remnant of Chapin & Gore, grinned sardonically. He was not at all concerned over Bertram's threat. It did not worry him. Ahead glittered glorious opportunity. He would go to Broncho House and take over. He'd take the twenty-five hundred a month, too, only, when the goods came down, he might take more. No use slaving in the desert at Broncho House. No use working his head off for the other fellow—for Bertram and Louthian and Hoehn—when there were towns in the south like Chihuahua City and Monterey and Mexico City.

Bob had always wondered how well a Mexican tailor could cut a suit of clothes. Maybe, after the wagonloads had been exchanged for *pesos,* he would just go down and see. There was nothing to prevent him, certainly not his conscience. He was so engrossed in the idea, in the visions of a rosy, albeit dishonest, future, that he failed to note the lanky gentleman who strolled into the Rajah.

The lanky man sought the bar and ordered whiskey. "Who is that?" the stranger asked when the drink was poured.

"Bob Roberts," the bartender answered. "Dandy Bob Roberts."

"Oh," said the lanky man, and drank. "I seen him talkin' to Bertram from up in Tucson." He put his right hand into his pocket and metal *clinked* faintly: silver dollars *clicked* against a small gold shield upon which was engraved: **TERRITORY OF ARIZONA. RANGERS**.

III

"KIDNAPPED"

Bob Roberts left Gila City the next morning. He wore his work clothes, a Colt, a Winchester on his saddle, and, as an afterthought, a .41 caliber Derringer, tucked into a vest pocket. Before he left, he tried to arouse Old Man Duggan, but without success. Duggan snored, rolled over, and snored some more, and Dandy Bob, noting that his liquor bottle was empty, knew Duggan was good for some time to come. So, without more ado, he saddled and rode southwest toward the end of the Dragoons and Broncho House. As he rode, he hummed a little tune, off key, pleased with himself and the world, and entirely unaware that the song he sang was "Annie Laurie".

Some two hours after Bob's departure, Gila City sat up, rubbed its eyes, and began the day's business.

The first transaction was accomplished at the Star Livery, which was also the stage station. Madame Tetri's accompanist and manager arranged passage for himself and the diva on the westbound stage. Madame Tetri had almost recovered from the shock to her artistic sensibilities and wished to shake the dust of Gila City from her shoes. The stage manager sympathetically booked the passengers.

Next in order was the advent of the lanky stranger at the livery barn. The barn boss was surly, due to the fact that his hostler, Raphael Sena, had not reported for work. "He was here yesterday when the stage left," the boss complained. "He was hangin' around Gene Bertram an' them other

Tucson fellers while they waited for the stage, an' I told him to go on about his business. I ain't saw him since. I'll get your horse in a minute."

"Has Bob Roberts been here this mornin'?" the lanky one asked.

"I seen him ridin' out of town when I come down to work," the liveryman said. "Just hold on to yourself, mister. Or if you want to, you can saddle your own horse."

The stranger wanted to. Within minutes he, also, was headed out of town, riding slowly and searching the ground, as does a man who cuts for sign.

Next in the sequence of events was the arrival of the stage for the west. Madame Tetri and her manager loaded themselves on, the stage pulled out; from the window of her cottage the Widow Fennessy saw it depart, catching a glimpse of its occupants. She sniffed disdainfully. So that woman was leaving town, was she? A good thing, too! The widow went to her kitchen. There, as she worked, her attitude softened. After all, Aloysius had gone to the rescue of a woman in distress. Perhaps his protestations had been true, perhaps he had simply obeyed his chivalrous nature and sought to protect all womanhood, with nothing personal involved. The widow sniffed away a tear, weakening because she was lonely and Old Man Duggan was so brave. Then she set about making gingerbread. One of Duggan's weaknesses—and he had many—was a pan of that brown stuff. Aloysius was sure to come hanging around some time in the course of the afternoon, and, when he had suffered a while, the widow would forgive him.

Duggan's plan for the day, however, did not include a visit to Mrs. Fennessy. When he wakened, he found himself with a splitting headache, an unusual thing, for whiskey did not ordinarily bother him. Moreover, when Duggan looked out, he saw that he had overslept. Dandy Bob was gone and so too was the stage Duggan had planned to take. His plans were knocked into a cocked hat and, surly as a sore-headed bear, he went downtown to get his breakfast liquor.

Two drinks fixed up his head but not his disposition. He wandered over to the Star Livery, learned that Roberts had been seen leaving town and that Raphael, who the barn boss cursed heartily, was absent from duty. Duggan then strayed back to the Rajah. He took another shot and sat down moodily. It appeared that Duggan would not be kidnapped this day. However, liquor got to work and fired his invention boiler, and, presently, the old man saw a way out.

He didn't need Dandy Bob and he didn't need the stage. He had the note to Widow Fennessy in his pocket. There was nothing to prevent his leaving town, hiring a Mexican to bring in the note and mail it, and then, in a few days, return with a story of escape from his kidnappers. Duggan's eyes brightened. He liked a lie nearly as well as he liked a drink and he would concoct a suitable tale. Moreover he knew where he could get a messenger and at the same time find a hide-out. Rancho Santisima was below the border, perhaps fifty miles from Gila City, and Duggan's friend, *Don* Filiberto, would not ask questions but would supply suitable hospitality. Duggan counted his money, estimated it to be enough, and, having purchased two quarts and his rations for the trip, went back to the adobe.

As shift boss of the Limerick Girl, Duggan had been affluent enough to keep a horse. The job was gone but the animal wasn't. Duggan saddled, collected a shotgun and a .45 Colt, and, having bestowed armament and rations on his saddle and person, mounted and headed south. He was bound for Rancho Santisima and, barring Apaches, the Sisneros bandits, or other accidents, would get there. Fortunately no marauding Indians were abroad, and, although Duggan did not know it, the brothers Sisneros were busy. Old Man Duggan himself had started the powder train that roused them to activity, for Luz and Chacon Sisneros, with certain of their following, were holding up the stage.

Ten miles out of Gila City, making heavy hauling up a grade, the stage came to an abrupt stop. The nigh leader fell in a tangle of harness, and, as the gunshot echoed and the guard and driver arose to offer resistance, a hail of lead swept the top of the vehicle. Driver and guard went down, both badly wounded, and the two passengers screamed in unison. Swarthy, big-hatted men, armed to the teeth, made their appearance. The Sisneros brothers, thoroughly coached and adding a new trick to their already overflowing bag, surrounded the vehicle.

They had gone to kidnap Old Man Duggan. Raphael Sena had posted them thoroughly and the Sisneros brothers, always with an eye on business, failed to see where they might not profit by Duggan's plan. But Duggan was not on the stage. When the passengers alighted, they comprised only a large, richly dressed, and important-appearing woman and a small, white-faced, and unimportant man. The Sisneros were in a quandary. Much Spanish was spoken.

Presently, however, a solution presented itself. Luz, the older brother, stated matters logically. They had come to kidnap, they would kidnap. They would take the large woman and let the small man go. The woman, who looked and doubtless was so wealthy and important, would be held for ransom. The man would go back to Gila City and get the money. These facts were communicated in halting English to the trembling manager. Despite her struggles Madame Tetri was hoisted and firmly bound upon a mule. The swarthy men departed. They had not been gone ten minutes when a lanky individual came loping up the grade.

The newcomer's first concern was for guard and driver. He bound up wounds while he listened to the manager's hysterical recital.

"Look," the lanky one commanded, interrupting, "you can ride, can't you? All right, you're goin' to anyhow. You go back to Gila City. Go straight to the stage stop. Tell 'em what happened. Get a posse started an' have 'em send a wagon out with the doctor. Tell 'em Bert Anstruther sent you. Bert Anstruther, get it? I'm a Territorial Ranger. Tell 'em I've followed these kidnappers an' that I'll leave plain sign for 'em to trail me by. Can you do that?" He moved efficiently to cut the harness from a mule.

It took more coaching but presently the diva's manager had the message letter perfect. Anstruther helped him mount and sent him on his way. Then turning again to the wounded, he inspected his handiwork. The guard was conscious.

"Go on," the guard ordered weakly. "Git them dirty rotten sons! Don't let 'em get away. Me and Jim'll make it through till Doc gets here."

Anstruther did not want to leave but he had done all he could. "They'll burn the breeze," he assured the guard. "An' that mule ain't loafin' on the way to town. They'll be here in two hours. Three maybe. Sure you'll be all right?"

The guard profanely reassured him and Anstruther rode off, heading along the plain trail left by the Sisneros. Three miles from the grade, where the crippled stage lay, the trail struck *malpais* and became obscure. Anstruther cursed wearily and began the slow process of working it out.

So, in the country west of Gila City, men moved about, each on his own business. Dandy Bob Roberts rode cheerfully, his journey to Broncho House nearing completion. Bert Anstruther searched through *malpais* for a hoof mark, an overturned rock, grass that had been bent by a passing horse.

Farther south than either of these, Old Man Duggan moved along, taking an occasional drink and still congratulating himself on his inventiveness. He reached the border, crossed it, and, as he lowered his bottle, his eyes caught the flicker of a dust cloud rising to the south.

Dust clouds might be caused by a number of things: cattle, horses, men, wind blowing. Duggan speculated briefly on the phenomenon and, thinking of contingencies, mentally marked the closest haven as Broncho House. If the dust were raised by bandits or Apaches, he would flee there, but, until he knew what was under the dust, there was no need to worry. He grunted and rode on.

Under the dust cloud Captain Ramón García of the *rurales* spoke cheerfully to his sergeant. The depredations of the brothers Sisneros had been forcibly called to the attention of Chihuahua's *gobernador* by *Don* Filiberto Paiz. The Republic of Mexico, as well as Arizona Territory, was weary, completely fed up with Luz and Chacon Sisneros. And Mexico, like Arizona, was doing something about it. Captain García's troop had spent the night at Rancho Santisima and now was scouting along the border, searching for the bandits. García, an excellent officer, was pleased with the detail. He spoke again to the sergeant and that worthy, half Yaqui and with eyes like an eagle, lifted in his stirrups and pointed north. Someone rode there, the sergeant said.

García trusted his sergeant's eyes. They would, he said, go and see. A brief order snapped and the dust cloud changed direction. Old Man Duggan did not note the change.

In Gila City the Widow Fennessy took gingerbread from the oven and mopped her sweating brow. A mule pounded past her cottage as she took out the second pan. Where, oh, where, was Aloysius? Time passed while the widow and the gingerbread grew cooler. A little posse of horsemen trotted out of town. A wagon rattled past, the driver plying the whip. There came a knock on the cottage door.

"Yis?" said the widow to the editor of the *Herald*.

"I'm collecting, Missus Fennessy," the editor said. "The Sisneros boys stopped the westbound stage and took Madame Tetri. They're holding her for ransom. A posse's gone out after them but, just in case they aren't caught, we're getting the ransom money ready. How much can I put you down for?"

"The Sisneros, is it?" demanded the widow. "Bad cess to 'um! Put me down for a hundred dollars. Wait, I'll bring ye the money!"

IV

" 'I'VE BEEN WAITIN' FOR YOU!' "

Dandy Bob Roberts, having nooned at a water hole, reached
Broncho House at three in the afternoon. He had a story ready.
He did not intend to conceal his identity but he planned to tell
Soldier Deutch that he, Dandy Bob, was on the dodge and
headed for Mexico. It was a good tale, well backed. Deutch
should be sympathetic with anyone fleeing from the law. Soldier
knew what it was to have a posse trailing him.

When Dandy Bob dismounted, he thought he recognized
one of the Mexicans and was not particularly interested. He
confronted the hostile faces cheerfully and asked for Soldier
Deutch.

El Soldado, one of the loungers said, was inside. Bob
walked into the house, pausing within the door to let his sight
grow accustomed to the gloom. He heard a soft voice behind
him say—*"Está aqui, Soldado."*—and, as his eyes adjusted to
the light, found himself staring at a gun. Behind the weapon
so competently held was a large man, a familiar man, the man
who Dandy Bob had hit at the concert, the lover of "Annie
Laurie".

"I been expectin' you, Roberts," the large man said.
"Take this gun offen him, Raphael." Dandy Bob felt the
weight of his pistol removed. "Sit down," the large man ordered. "You asked for Soldier Deutch. I'm him."

Dandy Bob sat down. He could feel, rather than hear, the
loafers slip into the room.

Deutch laughed harshly. "So you was comin' out here to take over my job," he rasped. "That's good, that is. You come walkin' in like a sheep. Raphael heard Bertram an' Louthian an' Hoehn talkin' at the stage depot after they propositioned you. They said you'd come, an' Raphael rode out to tell me. Dandy Bob Roberts! The tough *hombre* from Gila City! That's a laugh, that is!" Deutch lowered his weapon, glanced at it, and then slid it into his holster.

"When you goin' start takin' over?" he asked.

Dandy Bob did not answer. Neglected in his vest pocket, he had the medicine for Soldier Deutch, but he could not give it to him as yet. Deutch had put his gun away, but Bob knew he was still covered. There were plenty of men behind him. Tough men, too.

"Just goin' to walk in an' kick me out," Deutch said. "Why don't you get to kickin'?"

"Because," said Dandy Bob, "I ain't ready to."

"An' you won't ever be ready to." Deutch got up and walked over to confront his prisoner. "You ain't never goin' to kick me out because I'm goin' to kill you."

"So?" Bob said coolly. He had never in his life been in a closer place than this, nor, oddly enough, had he ever been more calm. Bertram, Louthian, and Hoehn had caused this trouble. Their big mouths, exercised on the stage platform in Gila City, had put him in this spot, and yet he was not particularly angry with them. Considering what he himself had planned, there was no cause for anger. Dandy Bob felt a faint regret that he could not carry out his scheme, but that was all. He would, when the time came, take Soldier with him. Maybe another. There were two shots in the Derringer.

"An' you hit me with a gun the other night," Deutch said. "You know, Roberts, it's goin' to be a pleasure to stop your clock. What in hell'd you hit me for?"

"Because you was raisin' hell an' I wanted to hear the concert," Dandy Bob answered.

"I wanted that woman to sing 'Annie Laurie'," Soldier announced. "That's a swell song. I used to know a girl that sung it. What you got against 'Annie Laurie'?"

"Nothin'," Bob answered honestly. "I was kind of hopin' she'd sing it for an encore myself."

"You was?" Soldier looked his disbelief. "Well, you'll never hear her sing it now."

"Neither will you," said Dandy Bob.

"That's right," Deutch said. "I . . . say, what's goin' on? What's all this, Raphael?"

There was a minor commotion behind Dandy Bob. Someone announced in Spanish that Luz and Chacon were coming. Deutch scowled. "You set still!" he warned Roberts. "Don't you say nothin'. I ain't done with you."

Dandy Bob sat still and Deutch went out. There were many voices outside. Then before Bob's startled eyes, a woman was pushed into the room—a big woman, a disheveled woman with her hat askew, and angry as a woman can get. Madame Simone Tetri faced her captors and the Middle West was in her voice.

"Damn you!" Madame Tetri swore. "You no-account, good-for-nothing, low-down. . . ." She continued in that vein. Opera stars, Dandy Bob thought calmly, were not as refined as they might be in their language.

It was Soldier Deutch who stopped the tirade. Soldier seized madame's arm and rasped: "Shut up!"

Miraculously Madame Tetri obeyed.

Now Dandy Bob had time for others than the woman. There were new arrivals in the room, all speaking Spanish. Bob heard of the stage's being stopped, of the shooting of the guard and driver, of the ransom demand sent to Gila City by the terrified manager. Soldier Deutch, having heard the report of the brothers Sisneros, stared at Roberts.

"Don't that beat hell!" he demanded, as one equal to another. "Now they've got the whole country comin' down on us."

"That's right," Bob Roberts agreed. "They'll not get away with this."

"I got to think," Soldier said. "I got to do some figurin'." He turned from Dandy Bob and issued orders. Madame Tetri was to be put into another room. So was Roberts. Soldier jerked his thumb at Dandy Bob. Rough hands seized Bob. He was hustled along the length of the room and through a door. Madame Tetri was thrust inside and the door closed. Beyond it, voices rose and fell in argument.

Madame Tetri's modish hat with drooping ostrich plumes lay limply on the floor. There were streaks of blonde or gray at the roots of madame's hair. Madame Tetri's face was contorted with anger. She kicked the door viciously.

"This," the madame announced, "is a hell of a note."

"Whereabouts are you from?" Dandy Bob asked.

"Chicago! And I wish I was there right now!"

Bob sat on the floor, leaving the bench for his companion. "It wouldn't be a bad place," he observed. "Better than this, anyhow." He was right about opera singers: their language was just not refined.

"What will they do with us?" Madame Tetri demanded.

"I don't know," said Dandy Bob. "You'll be all right, though. They won't hurt you." Thus reassured, Madame Tetri sat down.

Beyond the door, floods of Spanish welled back and forth, rising in waves, only to diminish. Bob, listening, caught some of it. Soldier Deutch was arguing that the woman should be turned loose and returned to Gila City. The Sisneros brothers, sold on the kidnapping idea, weren't having any. Ransom they wanted and ransom they would have! The odor of hot chili filtered through the door. There was the *clink* of iron on tin.

"Don't we eat?" Madame Tetri demanded.

"Not tonight," said Dandy Bob.

The light in the room, admitted through a small window, was dimming rapidly. Dusk had come. Outside, beyond the door, the argument resumed. The scent of burning tobacco seeped in under the door. Reminded, Dandy Bob felt for the makings.

"Roll me one," Madame Tetri ordered.

Bob Roberts rolled two cigarettes.

They were smoking companionably when the door opened and light streamed into the room. Soldier Deutch blocked the light. "Come on out," he commanded.

There was nothing to do but obey. Politely Bob stood aside for the lady to precede him. When they entered the main room of Broncho House, they found it nearly full.

Most prominent among the crowd were Luz and Chacon Sisneros, with Raphael Sena closely beside them. Soldier Deutch lined up with Dandy Bob. "I been tryin' to get 'em to let the woman go," he said, low-voiced. "They won't hear it. Lissen, if I make a break, will you get her out of here?"

"I'll try," Bob agreed. "I can't promise a thing."

Luz Sisneros snapped a command. He wanted Spanish spoken. Soldier Deutch obeyed. Here was the woman, he said. They could see for themselves she was valueless. But the *gringos* would be very, very angry because she had been taken. They would come; they would surely come.

Why then, Luz demanded, if the woman had no value, would the *gringos* pursue?

Because she was a singer, and a woman, Deutch explained. *Gringos* liked to hear her sing.

"*¡Cantá mujer!*" Luz interrupted. "*Caniá por mi.*"

"He wants you to sing," Bob said.

"Sing for these pigs?" Madame Tetri demanded. "I won't do it!"

Luz caught the word "pigs", and the woman's angry attitude. His face darkened. "*¡Canta!*" he snapped.

"Go on an' sing," Bob urged. "Don't make him mad. Sing 'Annie Laurie'."

"I won't . . . ," Madame Tetri began, and then, seeing the scowls on the faces about her: "All right. I'll sing."

"Good an' loud," Bob urged. "Let her roll."

Madame Tetri let her roll. "Annie Laurie" is a sentimental song, a song to be softly, tenderly sung, but not that night, not in Broncho House. "Maxwelton's braes are bonny" rang out like a giant bell, blasting, pealing. Eyes widened and mouths popped open. Under the cover of that mighty voice Bob Roberts whispered: "Give me a gun an' make your break."

"Not yet." Soldier Deutch's voice was equally soft. "Wait till she gets done."

". . . Where early fa's the dew. . . ."

A quarter mile from Broncho House, Daffyd ap Griffiths raised his head and listened. A song came to him across the desert, sweet, tempered by the distance. Daffyd got up on his feet and listened. Then, shaking his head in disbelief, he walked out and caught a grazing burro. He knew he was crazy but he would just go and see.

"An' for bonnie Annie Laurie, I'd lay me down an' dee." The song ended. Outside Broncho House a burro brayed, loud and raucous in the silence that had fallen. It was Daffyd's burro, greeting others of his ilk in the corral, but the occupants of Broncho House could not know that. They

132

simply knew that the bray meant someone was coming and that meant danger.

For an instant eyes were diverted from the singer and her companions. Dandy Bob seized the opportunity. "Now!" he snapped. "Give me that gun!"

Soldier Deutch was slow in complying. Perhaps the spell of the song still held him. He moved to obey, but too late. Raphael Sena, graduate of the fourth grade in the Sisters' School, interpreter *par excellence,* had not been diverted by the burro's bray. Raphael understood Bob's order and his gun snapped out and flamed. Soldier Deutch went down, shot through the head.

It was time for action now, time for the Derringer. It slid into Bob Roberts's hand, a little gun, a stubby gun, a gun for close and murderous work. The Sisneros were close. Luz went down, a hole between his eyes. Bob Roberts's stout left arm thrust Madame Tetri back through the door into the prison room. Chacon went down, his mouth a bloody mess, his neck snapped by the .41 slug. Bob dropped to the floor and swept up Soldier's fallen gun. Raphael Sena, caught by three loads in chest and belly, staggered in a circle, holding himself together.

Horses pounded outside. In the pandemonium of that lighted room Old Man Duggan thrust his bearded face. Duggan saw Roberts on the floor. Old Man Duggan's shotgun swept up and eighteen buckshot interfered with a man leveling off at Dandy Bob.

"Hold 'em, Bob!" Old Man Duggan shrilled and, drawing his Colt, fired again. He was whiskey brave, filled with liquid courage, but who knew that? The Sisneros gang and the men of Broncho House were suddenly between two fires. Nor was that all. Now others came. Here were uniforms.

"*¡Rurales!*" someone shrieked, and dived through a

window. There was no fight now, only panic that spread like wildfire. Old Man Duggan battled through the turmoil to Dandy Bob. He wheeled about and faced the room.

"My God!" Old Man Duggan panted. "I thought they was the Sisneros. I run into 'em on the border an' they taken a shot at me. I made a ride for here to get away. *Rurales* all the time."

The turmoil diminished. There were dead men on the floor and living men standing against the walls, their hands held high. A swarthy gentleman, his uniform dusty but unruffled, appeared before Dandy Bob and Duggan.

"*Señores . . . ,*" the swarthy man began, then stopped, for more horses were halting outside Broncho House.

Now there were new faces at the door, familiar faces: Jim Frazee, the Gila City postmaster; Simmons, who drove the mail buckboard; Charlie Hoyte from Freedom Hill; Watson, the assayer, and others. They crowded into the room, guns drawn, and among them was a tall stranger.

"Good gosh!" Old Man Duggan gasped, "everybody but the rangers."

The tall stranger grinned. "They're here, too, mister," he announced. "I'm a ranger. Where's the woman?"

In answer to the question, Madame Tetri appeared. She stood in the door behind Dandy Bob, poised there for an instant, making her entrance, and then with one swift step she reached Bob's side, her arms went about his neck, her lips to his cheek.

"My hero!" Madame Simone Tetri exclaimed. "My rescuer."

V

"REWARD FOR A HERO"

It took some small amount of time to sort matters out. Bert
Anstruther, representing the Territory of Arizona, and rein-
forced by his badge, forgathered with Captain Ramón García of
the *rurales*. García, sheathed with politeness, explained the presence of himself and his men in United States territory. He had
been, he explained, scouting along the boundary in search of
those *ladrónes,* the Sisneros brothers. His men had seen a rider
who, after approaching them at first, had turned and fled. They
had, of course, pursued, and all unwittingly crossed the border.
The mistake was understandable; the boundary was not well de-
fined. It should be better marked: *¿Qué no?*

At this point Old Man Duggan lost himself in the crowd.
He didn't know how close a look Captain García had had at
the fugitive, but old Duggan was taking no chances.

Anstruther, on his part, was equally polite and equally
firm. He understood *el señor capitán's* mistake perfectly, and
surely he would say nothing of it. Indeed, *el capitán* had been
most opportune, most efficient. He himself, Bert Anstruther
of the Arizona Rangers, complimented the *buen capitán*.
Anstruther said he had been on a similar mission. He had
been seeking the smugglers and the men who had kidnapped
a woman. That was a very serious thing in *america del norte*.
The good citizens of Gila City had also been hunting bandits.
They had joined forces and, hearing the sounds of firing,
come apace.

135

What, Captain García asked pointedly, was to be done with the prisoners?

Anstruther shrugged. They were doubtless citizens of the Republic of Mexico. He would place them in the *capitán's* tender care to be returned to their native land. The *rurale* captain smiled faintly and issued commands. The long room of Broncho House began to empty.

When García, his men, and prisoners were gone, Anstruther issued orders to those who remained. The bodies must be cared for, but Anstruther would come back with laborers and take care of the matter at a later date. The immediate necessity was to return Madame Tetri to Gila City. There were horses to catch, a wagon to be hitched, a ride to make. Men departed on these errands and Anstruther turned to Dandy Bob and stared at him, hard.

Dandy Bob and Duggan were together, but Madame Tetri had found a kindred soul. Daffyd ap Griffiths, he whose burro had brayed so opportunely, was caring for her, fussing over her, bringing her water and *aguardiente* in a gourd. Madame sipped her mixture of brandy and water daintily while Daffyd stood by with worshipping eyes.

"How come you to be down here?" Anstruther demanded of Dandy Bob. "Just scouting around?" His voice and questions were abrupt, but the ranger's eyes were friendly.

"Just scoutin' around," Dandy Bob agreed.

"Handy, this scoutin' business," Anstruther commented. "Of course, I was lookin' for smugglers in the first place. I guess we got 'em all. They was goin' to arrest Bertram, Hoehn, an' Louthian in Tucson today. We been investigatin' them quite a while. Them an' Soldier Deutch was ramroddin' the deal this side of the line."

"I guess they were," Bob agreed.

Faintly, from far to the south, shots sounded, the rattle of what might have been a volley. Both men listened.

"*Ley del fuego*," Anstruther said. "Well . . . that's the way they do it. Bad people to get mixed up with."

"Mexicans?"

"Smugglers. Deutch an' Bertram an'. . . ."

"Not Deutch," Dandy Bob stated. "Deutch was all right."

Watson, the assayer, thrust his head into the room. "We got the wagon ready," he announced.

So, from Broncho House, the men of Gila City made their departure, riding as escort about the wagon containing Madame Simone Tetri.

For a time Daffyd ap Griffiths walked by the wagon, then, reluctantly, worship still in his eyes, branched off to go back to his camp in the dry wash, back to his lonely prospecting in the hills. But with him Daffyd carried a greater treasure than he would ever find with pick or rock hammer, for Madame Tetri had scrawled her name upon a piece of paper and Daffyd had it in his pocket. **All my affection to a true lover of music. Simone Tetri.**

If ever he had grandchildren, Daffyd would show them that.

The night was long and the wagon bumped. Dandy Bob rode close and Madame Tetri, leaning out, beckoned him closer. "Don't tell them," she whispered. "Don't tell them I'm from Chicago."

"No danger. I won't," Dandy Bob assured, and pulled away again.

Everyone had his secrets, Dandy Bob thought, even opera singers. Certainly Dandy Bob had his. Anstruther knew why Bob had ridden to Broncho House; he must know, for, when he spoke of Bertram and those others, his meaning had been plain. The ranger had warned Bob Roberts to keep his mouth shut. Bob intended to. He grunted his disappointment, thinking of what might have been. In a way, he was lucky, a lot luckier than Soldier Deutch or the Sisneros brothers. However, that was small consolation. The smuggling business was blown up, what with men in jail, and men dead, and a wonderful opportunity had gone glimmering. He would never make a cent out of this business, Bob thought.

As the sun rose, the little cavalcade reached Gila City, and Gila City turned out to welcome them. The tale was told and re-told by every man who had gone out, and once more Dandy Bob Roberts was a hero, with Duggan a close second. Once again Madame Tetri sought the solitude of the New York Hotel to recuperate, but, before she left, she again embraced her rescuer and kissed his cheek. Gila City enjoyed that. There were drinks for the posse men, drinks for Dandy Bob. There would have been drinks for Old Man Duggan save that, before he had taken more than one or two, the Widow Fennessy appeared and led him away.

By ten o'clock the crowd had thinned, each going about his business. It was then that Old Man Duggan found Dandy Bob in the Rajah.

Bob was tired. He sat wearily in his accustomed place beside the poker table, trying to get up courage to ride home, unsaddle his horse, and go to bed.

"You know what, Bob?" Old Man Duggan planked himself down in a chair. "The widow baked me two pans of gingerbread."

"She did!" Bob said. "Want a drink?"

"Nope." Duggan's air was virtuous. "I quit drinkin'. Anyhow, till the gingerbread's gone. You ain't goin' to have to kidnap me, Bob. I'm in good with the widdy again."

"Kidnap you?" Weary as he was, Dandy Bob came half out of the chair.

"Like you said the other day," Duggan reminded. "When we was talkin', remember? You said, if I got kidnapped, it would make the widdy strong for me again."

Bob relaxed. Vaguely he recalled the conversation in the saloon.

"I had it figured out," Duggan stated complacently. "First I was goin' to have you kidnap me an' blame it on the Sisneros boys. Then I decided I'd just kidnap myse'f. But we won't have to now. I just come around to tell you about it." Duggan got up.

"Wait a minute," Bob Roberts ordered. There had been a kidnapping and the Sisneros had done the work. There was more to this than met the eye.

"I promised Vi'let I'd be right back," Duggan said, and headed for the door.

He was gone and Dandy Bob got up to follow, but more men came in, advancing toward him. He reseated himself wearily. More men to ask questions, to exclaim, to praise him, to offer drinks. He wished they would go away. All he wanted was sleep.

The editor of the *Gila City Herald* led the little group, and the editor looked important, as will a man who has a project on his mind. He paused portentously in front of the table and cleared his throat.

"You're a hero, Bob," the editor announced. "Gila City is proud of you. We took up a collection when we learned that Madame Tetri had been kidnapped. We considered it a civic duty to pay her ransom if she wasn't found and released. Now it won't be necessary to use the money that way. We all talked it over among ourselves and we decided to present it to you. We want you to buy some memento of the occasion, something that will always remind you of the esteem in which you are held by your fellow citizens."

The editor could be flowery in speech as well as with his ink. He placed a roll of bills on the table.

"That's more'n six hundred bucks, Bob," a man behind the editor announced.

Dandy Bob looked at the money, and then at the editor. The editor stood poised, like a man ready to pounce. Bob looked at the money again, slowly shaking his head in disbelief. It wasn't so. It just couldn't happen.

"Well?" the editor said. "Haven't you anything to say?"

"Yeah," said Dandy Bob, and pocketed the bills. "I have. I sure have. Somebody around here is crazy. I think it's me."

Gila's Forty-Rod Justice

I

"A HELL OF A FUNNY JOKE"

It took more than an ordinary occurrence to upset Gila City. When the border town wakened in the morning, it never knew what to expect. It might be a killing that served as a breakfast topic, or, perhaps, a new silver strike. Stage robberies were common; Apache raids roused only passing interest. Gila City was blasé and, generally, tough enough to take care of whatever turned up, but the day after election the news was enough to jolt the town's equanimity. Old Man Duggan had been elected justice of the peace and, furthermore, *intended to serve*.

The whole thing was a joke. Bliss Cassidy, who had recently purchased the Rajah Saloon, started the ball rolling. Bliss possessed both a reputation as a gunman and a sense of humor, and on election morning he announced to his bartender that he intended to vote for Duggan as J.P.

"Damned ol' drunkard ought to be good for somethin'," Bliss commented. "I been here a month an' all I ever seen him do was get drunk an' tell lies about fightin' Apaches. Let's frame him. If we elect him J.P., he'll scratch an' crawl to get out of servin'."

The bartender, an older resident than his employer, looked dubious. "Duggan teams around a lot with Dandy Bob Roberts," the bartender said. "Him an' Bob are kind of partners. I don't know will Bob like it if we frame up the old man."

"An' who is Bob Roberts?" Cassidy demanded. "You-all

around here act like he was a tin god or somethin'. I ain't afraid of Roberts an' I'll never see the day when I will be afraid of him. I'm goin' to vote for Duggan an' spread the word around. Anyhow, Roberts is out of town. He's went to Tucson."

The bartender shrugged. Fools rush in where angels fear to tread, and, if something happened to Bliss Cassidy, the bartender figured he could still get a job. "Suit yourself," he said.

Cassidy passed the word around. Gila City's sense of humor was macabre and in the eyes of the border town it was possible for a man to die and be funny at the same time. The idea of electing Duggan to the office of J.P. appealed and tickled Gila City's risibilities. Duggan could hardly read or write and no one would be fool enough to go the old sot's bond. By six o'clock, when the polls closed, two hundred humorists had voted for Old Man Duggan.

Dandy Bob Roberts, returning home from Tucson, heard the news the day following. He accepted it calmly. Always immaculate, he cleaned up and changed clothes, then went to call on the Widow Fennessy.

The widow, formerly Gila City's washwoman, owned the Limerick Girl, one of the richest silver properties in the district. Dandy Bob and Duggan had found the lost vein in the mine and restored the property to the widow. Moreover, the Widow Fennessy was toying with the idea of marrying Duggan, always providing that she could not find someone more suitable. Dandy Bob left the widow's vine-covered cottage and word seeped out over the town. The Widow Fennessy intended to make Duggan's bond. The old man was going to serve in the office to which he had been elected. Consternation reared its ugly head.

A committee of sober citizens headed by Postmaster Jim

Frazee and including Henry Hinkle, the defeated candidate
for justice of the peace, called upon Duggan and Dandy Bob.
Hinkle was a comparative newcomer to Gila City, having established a private bank in the town some six months prior to
election day. Hinkle, about as garrulous as an egg, was a small
man with a big, bald head. His candidacy had been advocated
by the Temperance League of which he was a member and
leading light. He hovered in the background while Frazee
stated the committee's business.

Duggan was sleeping off his post-election drunk but Bob
Roberts was wide awake and listened carefully to what Frazee
had to say. When the postmaster finished, Dandy Bob replied
definitely and to the point.

"You elected Duggan J.P.," Bob told the committee, "and
he's goin' to serve. Missus Fennessy thinks that bein' justice
is a dignified job an' she's makin' the bond. Her an' Duggan
are goin' to be married, you know. An' I'm backin' Duggan to
the limit. For my money, he's just what the town needs, an', if
somethin' should happen to him, I'd know where to look."

Mr. Roberts favored each of the committee with a stare.
The committee retired with no more ado. They all knew Bob
Roberts. They knew that he wore the best clothes in the territory, that his shirts were the most immaculate, his broadcloth
coat the finest, his boots the most high-polished, his Stetson
hat the best. They also knew that he wore a walnut-handled
Colt for business reasons only. Gila City had seen conclu-
sions tried with Bob Roberts and helped bury the triers. No
one wanted to buck Dandy Bob.

When Frazee and his fellows were gone, Dandy Bob sat
down and looked fondly at the sleeping Duggan. Visions of financial solvency filled Bob's mind. With Duggan as J.P. and
with Bob backing him, things were picking up. There would
be fines to collect and Bob would split those fines with

Duggan. There would be favors that the J.P. could dispense—at a price, of course. Manna, that was the way it looked to Bob, just plain manna dispensed by Gila City. Duggan snored and rolled over on his back.

Down at the Rajah Saloon, Bliss Cassidy heard the news and grunted. "So what if he is goin' to serve?" Bliss demanded. "That's all the better. The town will be wide open an' nothin' to stop it. Come on to the bar. Drinks are on the house!"

Both Bliss Cassidy and Dandy Bob Roberts were doomed to disappointment. Duggan, sobering from his drunk, went to call on the Widow Fennessy. He returned to Bob's adobe a chastened and wiser man. The widow had her ideas as to how a justice of the peace should comport himself and she had given Duggan a thorough orientation.

Old Man Duggan selected his ten-gauge shotgun from the arms rack on the wall and put twelve loaded shells in his coat pocket. He combed his hair, trimmed his beard, washed his face—not neglecting his ears—and stepped out to do his duty. The first man he fell foul of was Bliss Cassidy.

Bliss was standing in the door of the Rajah. Bliss was a tobacco chewer and, as Duggan approached, let go a gout of brown juice. The tobacco splashed on the boardwalk under the Rajah's wooden awning and Mr. Cassidy found himself staring into the twin barrels of the ten-gauge.

"Spittin' on the sidewalk," Duggan announced. "That's ten dollars' fine."

Dandy Bob Roberts used the Rajah for a hang-out when he was in town. Hearing Duggan's voice, he came hurriedly along the length of the room.

Bliss Cassidy exploded. "Ten dollars!" he shrilled. "That's my sidewalk . . . it belongs to me. I can spit on it if I want to! Why you old. . . ."

Eighteen buckshot tore the wooden framing from the top of the door, effectively discouraging Cassidy's speech. The shotgun, one barrel still loaded, centered again. "An' twenty-five dollars for contempt," Duggan snapped. "I'm J.P. an' I aim to run this town right. Pay me now, or else!"

There was no doubt but that the old man meant what he said. The buckshot had wrought havoc with the door frame. Bliss Cassidy paid.

Duggan, receiving the bills with his free hand, put them in his pocket. "An' you better get that door fixed," he warned. "It's unsightly, all splintered up that-a-way. I aim to have a neat town, too." He walked on down the street, his back straight, the shotgun across his arm, his beard waving in the little breeze. Bliss Cassidy retired with Bert Axtell to the bar and there found Dandy Bob.

"Good joke, ain't it?" Bob asked blandly. "Duggan bein' justice of the peace, I mean."

His answer was a scowl.

Logically Mr. Roberts expected to collect half the fine that Duggan had assessed, but, like Bliss Cassidy, he received a surprise. Bob approached the old man on the subject that night when they prepared for bed, and Duggan refused him.

"You an' me are pardners, all right," Duggan admitted, "but not in this J.P. business. I was elected an' the widdy made my bond. The widdy says, if I make good, she'll marry me an' no questions asked. She's done sent off for a law book an' she says I got to save the fines an' build a jail. She says, if I get a hundred dollars, she'll put up the rest an' we can buy that ol' cell they had in Tucson. I ain't goin' to split with you, Bob, an' that's that."

"You wouldn't last thirty minutes if I wasn't behind you," Dandy Bob snapped. "Somebody would stop your clock, only they're afraid of me."

"I ain't so sure," Duggan answered complacently. "I'm pretty good with a shotgun. An' you know what, Bob? The widdy says, if I'll quit drinkin', she'll make me a pan of gingerbread every day. I'm goin' to cut down on my liquor."

Bob Roberts, deposed kingmaker, grunted his unbelief. "If I just say the word . . . ," he began.

"But you won't," Duggan interrupted calmly. "You already declared yourse'f to Frazee an' them, an' you rubbed it into Cassidy today. You got to stay with me now or else back down, an', if you back down, you're done."

There was truth in the statement. Dandy Bob Roberts pulled off his boots and turned in.

So began a reign of terror in Gila City, at least insofar as the sporting element was concerned. The law book arrived in due time. The fact that it was a codification of Vermont statutes, circa 1867, made no difference. The widow read the law to Gila City. No more did pistols pop cheerfully at night; no more did cowpunchers ride their horses into the Rajah or the Mint or any of the other saloons; no more did miners from the Limerick Girl or the Silver Dollar or those other shafts that brought forth wealth sleep off their pay-day drunks where they fell.

Duggan amassed his hundred dollars in three days and so pleased Violet Fennessy that she contributed five times as much. Laborers began the erection of an adobe and the little iron cell was freighted down from Tucson. A month after Duggan's election Gila City had both a justice of the peace and a jail.

II

"BROTHER RAT"

It must not be supposed that the drinking, gambling, stage-robbing, cattle-rustling portion of Gila City accepted Duggan's reign with equanimity. Only the fact that Dandy Bob Roberts was believed to be behind the old man kept Duggan alive. Duggan wandered the streets with his shotgun, finding and fining offenders and leaving a trail of wrath in his passage, and complaints poured about Bob's ears. Men pleaded with him to call off Duggan, but to no avail.

Realizing, as Duggan had said, that he could not back down from the stand he had taken, Bob stared stony-faced at the complainers and gave them no solace. He was having a run of luck at the faro table and so appeared prosperous. The natural conclusion was that Bob was splitting the fines with the J.P. and he became as heartily hated as was Duggan. Bob could stand the hatred—it did not bother him—but it hurt to see opportunities for money-making pass. Periodically he broached ideas to Duggan, only to be met by an unwonted and uncompromising rectitude. About the time the new jail was completed, a matter arose that momentarily took Bob's mind off his troubles with Duggan.

One of the things that irked Bob Roberts was the lack of laundry facilities in his hometown. As long as the Widow Fennessy had toiled at her tubs, Bob's linen shirts had been things of beauty, but with the widow freed by the wealth of the Limerick Girl, the shirts assumed a gray and soiled appearance. Bob tried one washwoman after another, to no avail. His complacency suffered accordingly, for who can be a dandy with a dingy shirt? Bob was at low ebb when Wong T'seng entered upon the stage of Gila City.

Wong came in by freighter, stowed away in the body of a wagon beneath a wagon sheet. His discovery aroused his conveyers to wrath and two teamsters were about ready to work him over with a neck yoke when Duggan, attracted by the flow of profanity, arrived. Duggan's shotgun discouraged the neck yoke, and the freighters stood by while the old man pronounced judgment.

"Charged with bein' a Chinaman an' lackin' vis'ble means of support," Duggan announced. "I reckon you're guilty. That's ten dollars or ten days in the *jusgado*."

Wong did not have ten cents, much less ten dollars, and Duggan hailed him off to incarceration. *En route* to the jail the pair met Dandy Bob.

A Chinese meant one thing to Bob Roberts: laundry. He inquired as to Wong's status, learned that Wong was familiar with the mysteries of tubs and starch, and forthwith paid the fine.

"You're goin' to wash clothes . . . my clothes, to start with," Bob told the refugee. "Come on."

Wong followed his rescuer to the Widow Fennessy's cottage.

"Sure," the widow agreed sympathetically when she had heard the story, "my old tubs an' irons an' such are down in the shack by the river. The pore thing is welcome to 'em."

So it came about that Wong T'seng was established and, under Bob's protection, thrived. Within a week Bob's shirts shown in all their pristine whiteness and gladdened his heart. Within ten days Wong had all the laundry he could do. And he was not molested. Bob Roberts saw to that. No one cared to challenge him.

Although the laundry business thrived, Bob made no progress with Duggan. That gentleman was riding the crest, enforcing the law and having a fine time. Nor could anything Bob said change his queer honesty. The widow backed Duggan, Duggan enjoyed himself, and Bob was left out in the cold. He got the two together and spoke his mind.

"If it wasn't for me, Duggan wouldn't be J.P.," Bob stated. "He wouldn't last ten minutes. The only reason he gets by is that folks think I'm backin' him."

At that, Duggan swelled angrily, but the widow took the play. "It's me that backs Duggan," she refuted. "Didn't I go his bond? Of course, I did. An' I read the law book to him. G'wan with your big head, Bob Roberts. Me and Aloysius don't need ye."

"All right," Bob answered angrily, "if you don't need me then get along without me. I'm goin' to Tucson an' stay a while. Maybe I'll go on East, I don't know. When I'm gone, see how well you get along!"

He had an idea that Duggan would back down, but Duggan didn't. The widow patted Duggan's shoulder and Duggan bristled.

"Go on to Tucson, then," he said. "Vi'let's right. We don't need your backin'."

There was nothing for Bob to do but make good. He packed his clothes and engaged passage on the Tucson stage. Duggan came down to see him off, and the editor of the *Gila City Herald* and Jim Frazee were also present.

"How long will you be gone?" the editor asked, while the stage teams were being changed.

"I don't know," Bob answered. "Quite a while, I reckon." He glanced with malice at Duggan. "Hope you get

151

along all right while I'm away."

Duggan flinched a little, for the widow was not present and he was weakening. But the editor laughed.

"Oh, Duggan will do all right," he said. "Don't worry about Duggan. Everybody knows that, if Duggan got in trouble, you'd come back, an', anyhow, the town's behind Duggan, ain't it, Jim?"

Frazee nodded. "That's right," he agreed. "You know, when Duggan was elected, I thought we'd fooled ourselves, but now that he's took hold, I'm satisfied."

Duggan swelled visibly and Bob Roberts mounted to the top of the stage. The driver clucked to his teams and the stage rattled away. Bob did not look back. In the light of what Frazee and the editor had said, his trip seemed hardly worthwhile. For the first time since the election, Bob began to doubt that he, and he alone, was responsible for the old man's success.

Frazee, Duggan, and the editor were not the only ones that watched the stage leave. Bert Axtell and Bliss Cassidy, standing in front of the Rajah, saw the passage of the vehicle and noted the passenger on its top.

"There goes Bob Roberts," Cassidy said with satisfaction, "an' there goes Duggan's backin'. Now what is there to keep me from blowin' that old fool apart?"

"Nothin'," said Axtell, "except Gila City."

"What do you mean?" Cassidy demanded, leading the way into the saloon.

"I mean," Axtell said, "that the town's gettin' behind Duggan. All these storekeepers an' mine owners an' such are backin' him. I get around, Bliss, an' listen to the talk. There's lots of people in this town are pretty well satisfied with Duggan. They ain't sure of him yet, but, as long as he keeps goin' the way he has, they'll back him."

"That kind of backin' don't count," Cassidy said scornfully. "That ain't shootin' backin'. Roberts is gone an' I'm goin' to take that ol' fool down a peg. Finin' me for spittin' on my own sidewalk! Him an' that Widow Fennessy think they own the place."

"Bliss," Axtell said, squinting at the liquor Cassidy set out, "how would you like to take Duggan an' the widow an' Bob Roberts, too, an' do it so nobody could touch you?"

"I'd like it fine," Cassidy answered promptly, "but how?"

"I been thinkin'," Axtell said. "The way to hurt a man is through the pocketbook. Without Missus Fennessy an' Bob Roberts, Duggan ain't nothin'. Roberts is gone . . . nobody knows for how long. Now then . . . did you know that Mike Fennessy died intestate?"

"So what?"

"So Mike never made a will, that's what. His estate was never probated. I've looked up the records in Tucson. The Widow Fennessy just took over the Limerick Girl."

"What's wrong with that?" Cassidy stared curiously at his companion.

"Nothin's wrong with it. But there might be. Suppose somebody turned up with a claim on the estate . . . a brother, say. That would tie the mine up in litigation. There'd be a lawyer's fees for me an' the brother would likely get a share of the property."

"Mike Fennessy never had a brother that I heard of."

"He could have one, though." Axtell's two gold teeth glinted as he grinned knowingly. "You've been around, Bliss. You ought to know some big Irishman we could hire. I'll pump the widow an' find out what I can about Mike's folks. Then we fix our man up with letters an' such an' he blows in here an' puts up a claim for the Limerick Girl. He'll be supposed to have grubstaked Mike, see?"

"I know a man," Cassidy said. "Used to run a place on the Barbary Coast in Frisco. Him an' me have been in some things together. But the Fennessys come from the East, didn't they?"

"Boston, I think," Axtell answered. "That won't make any difference. Your man can say he come from Boston, can't he?"

Cassidy nodded. "We'll need some money," he observed. "This guy ain't cheap."

"Half the Limerick Girl is worth spendin' some money to get," Axtell retorted.

Cassidy pondered. "I ain't too flush right now," he said. "I owe a big liquor bill in Tucson an' my games ain't doin' so good. Roberts, damn him, has been takin' the faro bank."

"You get the money an' I'll go to Tucson an' line up what we need," Axtell said. "I can get the dope on the Limerick Girl an' the Fennessys, an' get the letters an' such written. Then you go to San Francisco an' see your man. Have him come in from the East. How about it?"

"I'll have to borrow," Cassidy said. "I wonder. I'll go see Hinkle. He loans money an' he don't talk. The Rajah's clear an' that might be money enough. By glory, Bert, we'll do it! I'd give all I got to be even with Duggan an' that blame' widow. I only wish I could get Roberts, too!" Cassidy chewed on that thoughtfully.

"Why not?" Axtell shrugged. "I'll be in Tucson an' there's men in the Old Pueblo that would settle Bob Roberts for fifty bucks."

III

"SIGNED LEAD SLUG"

Duggan's complacency, following Dandy Bob's departure, lasted three days. At the end of that time he felt like a man with a wooden leg who knows somebody is sawing. His dictum, heretofore met with prompt compliance, began to receive less respectful treatment and he was favored with plenty of hard looks.

For a week Duggan ran his bluff, patrolling with his shotgun, eating gingerbread at the widow's, and inspecting the jail, but he knew he was walking on quicksand. Dandy Bob's reputation and Dandy Bob's gun were far away, and Duggan missed them. He grew more and more nervous, and presently began to pull in his horns.

No more, when disorder threatened, was Duggan Johnny on the spot. When a quarrel flared up between drunks, Duggan did not arrive until others had separated the contestants and peace was restored. If a pistol popped, Duggan went the other way. At first this was hardly noticeable, Gila City as a whole not realizing that the reins were relaxed, then it began to show and there was talk.

Hearing the talk, the Widow Fennessy lectured Duggan and he braced up a bit. He collected some fines and delivered some lectures on civic virtue, but it was all too apparent that he picked his spots. The known hardcases were let strictly alone and only minor offenders came under Duggan's observation.

"He's losin' his nerve," Jim Frazee commented to

Watson, the assayer. "Now that Bob Roberts is gone, Duggan's backin' down. Maybe we should've put Hinkle in office, after all."

"Hinkle still wants it," Watson answered. "Get Duggan to resign an' the mayor can appoint Hinkle."

"We'll give Duggan a little more time," Frazee decided. "He done pretty good for a while. Maybe he'll pick up again."

But Duggan did not pick up. He quarreled with the widow, quit eating gingerbread, and went on a straight liquid diet. To cap it all, after Bob Roberts had been absent for a month, the westbound stage deposited a large, black-bearded gentleman in Gila City, a man who spoke with a brogue and who announced to all and sundry that he was Pat Fennessy, Mike's brother, and that he had come on business. Perforce Duggan was present when Pat called upon Mike Fennessy's relict.

The widow received Pat in her parlor. She had dressed for the occasion, powdered and corseted herself, and it was plain that she made an impression. Pat, accompanied by Bert Axtell, exhibited two letters purporting to be in Mike Fennessy's handwriting, and in the text of each was plainly mentioned the fact that Pat had grubstaked Mike.

"I dunno," the widow stated. "Mike nivver spoke of havin' a brother. He come from Boston, true enough, but it seems like he'd have said somethin' about you to me."

"He wouldn't," Pat Fennessy said. "Of course, he wouldn't. Whin Mike an' me was broths of bhoys I was always cuttin' him out with the gurls. Sure, with a fine, good-lookin' woman like yourself, Mike would keep his mouth shut. He'd be afraid to show you me picture even, for fear of what would happen." Pat stroked his curling mustache and swelled his chest, eyeing the widow meanwhile.

"An' if I'd seen *your* picture," Pat continued, "I'd been in

Gila City long before this."

The widow bridled and flushed and Bert Axtell took matters in hand. "Your husband's estate was never probated," he said. "My client has obtained a restraining order on the Limerick Girl and attached all bank deposits while we call for an accounting. You're entitled to that information, Missus Fennessy."

"An' what will I do now?" demanded the widow.

"Get a lawyer," said Duggan. He had better kept his mouth shut. All eyes were turned on him.

"An' you a justice of the peace an' let this happen to your own *feeancee!*" the widow snapped. "A foine justice you are. Get out!"

Duggan left hastily. The widow wept, and Pat was restrained from comforting her only by Axtell's quick action. Axtell got his man out of the cottage and upbraided him as they walked to the Rajah.

"See here," Bert Axtell snapped, "you're supposed to be sore at the widow. You're supposed to be here to collect what's yours from the Fennessy estate. An' the first thing you do is act like you wanted to make love to her."

"An' why not?" the pseudo-Pat demanded. "Let me tell you, Axtell . . . you an' Bliss have went about this wrong. The easiest way to get hold of all that mine an' the money is to marry the gurl, an' I'm just the lad that can do it."

Axtell glanced sharply at his companion. "After you've tied up her mine an' her bank account? You're crazy!"

"I could do it." The false Fennessy waved the objection aside. "I know wimmen."

"Don't go gettin' ideas about double-crossin' Bliss an' me," Axtell warned. "You've been paid for this job. If it was to leak out that you are from San Francisco an' that your name's O'Hara, Gila City would hang you."

"An' you alongside me," the false Fennessy stated. "Don't forget, if you talk, I talk. Whereabouts in this dump of a town can a man get his washin' done? I've got a lot of dirty clothes."

"Down at the chink's," Axtell said, and gave directions. "Here's the hotel. You go on to your room an' stay out of sight. There ought to be a deputy down from Tucson to serve them papers on the widow. I don't want you around."

They parted then, Axtell going directly to the Rajah where he consulted with Bliss Cassidy.

"Why, damn him!" Cassidy snapped. "If he does that, I'll shoot him myself. O'Hara better not try to double-cross me!" He brooded a moment before he spoke again. "What did you do about Bob Roberts, up in Tucson?"

Axtell grinned all across his foxy face. "Roberts is taken care of," he answered. "We ought to be hearin' about him just any time. There's the Tucson stage now!" Followed by Cassidy, he hastened to the door. The Tucson stage was stopping in front of the Star Livery and a passenger alighted.

"McMain," Axtell said. "He's deputy sheriff, come down to serve the papers on the widow. He's getting off it now."

"That calls for a drink," Cassidy announced. "Come on." They turned back to the bar.

If Bliss Cassidy and Bert Axtell had waited a moment longer, they would have seen Dandy Bob Roberts step out of the stage and join the deputy sheriff.

It had taken considerable thought and a combination of circumstances to cut short Bob Roberts's visit to Tucson. Arriving in that town, he had conducted himself with style and discretion. His constant companion had been Frank McMain who, besides being a deputy, was Bob's good friend. Mr. Roberts had been made welcome by the gamblers and other lights of the Old Pueblo and they had striven earnestly, but without success, to take his money. Dandy Bob had enjoyed an unusual run of luck and it had seemed that whatever he turned to paid a profit. As he had turned to faro, poker, and monte, the Tucson gamblers had suffered.

Despite his luck, Mr. Roberts was not happy for little or no news arrived from Gila City. The explosion Bob awaited for did not occur. Those casual travelers who came from the town to the south spoke of no upheavals, no difficulties. From their reports, Dandy Bob had received the idea that Duggan was getting along all right. This had irked him and made him a little reckless. Indeed, so lacking was he in caution that he had gotten into a game that lasted two nights and a day.

It had been a big game, square as a die, and with a great deal of money involved. There had been two professionals playing, Bob and one other, while the other four players had represented the cattle, mining, transportation, and mercantile industries. Groome Hance of Sherry & Hance, had been the big loser, and, in the thirty-fourth hour of poker, Groome had drawn a pair to go with three of a kind and set about recouping his losses. The only man who had stayed with him had been Dandy Bob Roberts. They had raised and re-raised, for it was a no-limit game.

"I'm behind," Mr. Hance had stated, "an' I'm sittin' here with a collection of cards that needs encouragement. I know it's table stakes, Bob, but I'd like to make an added entry. I've got an invoice an' sight draft here on liquor we sold Bliss Cassidy down in your town. It amounts to two thousand dollars. I'd like to enter it against about two stacks of them blue chips you're hoardin'. That is, if you're willin'."

Bob, who had gazed upon the smiling countenance of four queens, had been willing. The Cassidy draft and invoice had gone into the pot, had been called, and the showdown had come.

Mr. Hance had arisen in disgust. "That cleans me," he had observed, "cleaner than a picked chicken. If you have trouble collectin' that draft, let me know, Bob. I'll make it good. Gentlemen, I'm through. Poker's too fast for me this time."

Two hours later the game had broken up and Dandy Bob had retired. He had been aroused by a pounding on his door. When he had opened it, Frank McMain had come in.

"I'm goin' down to Gila City," the deputy had announced. "I come to tell you, Bob. I've got to serve a restraining order on the Widow Fennessy an' stop her operatin' the Limerick Girl. There's an attachment on her bank account here, too. Mike Fennessy's brother has turned up an' he's askin' for an accounting of Mike's estate. It never went through probate court an' the widow's in a hell of a mess."

Bob Roberts had yawned and stretched. "So?" he had said sleepily.

"The widow's a friend of yours," McMain had said. "I thought you'd want to know."

"Let Duggan look after it," Dandy Bob had said. "Him an' the widow claim they don't need me."

Bob had turned over and hidden his head under the pillow. McMain had waited a moment and then had gone on. After the deputy had departed, Bob had removed the pillow. Maybe—just maybe—he ought to go home. Maybe he ought to lend a hand. Then, recalling his last interview, he had steeled himself.

Thirty minutes after McMain's call, being in bed, his eyes closed and asleep to all appearances, worn out by the thirty-six hours of poker he had played, Dandy Bob had heard feet scrape softly on the balcony outside his window. He had slid a hand up under his pillow and waited. Some of the Tucson gamblers might be seeking to recoup their losses.

The slight noise had ceased; there had come a minor *thump,* and Dandy Bob, sitting bolt upright, had presented his Colt. By the window a very frightened, brown-skinned gentleman had dropped his knife and turned to escape.

"Alto," Bob had snapped.

The intruder had paused, gasping. Bob had gotten out of bed. "Thought you'd sneak in an' rob me, didn't you?" he had growled. "You're due to be a dead Mexican."

There had been no doubt in the intruder's mind that Bob's prophecy would come true. He had dropped to his knees and began to plead. Sorting words out of the babble, Bob had learned that his visitor was without stain and blameless, that he had not come to rob, but had been hired to end life.

"Who hired you?" Bob had demanded. "Spill it!"

The swarthy man had sworn that he did not know his employer's name. By all the saints, he had sworn it. But he had described the man. Small he was, and with the face of a fox, and with two gold teeth. *"Dos dientes del oro."*

Somewhere in Bob's memory two gold teeth had cropped up. He could not recall at once where he had seen them, but seen them he had. He had hauled the intruder to his feet, shoved him out the window, and kicked. The balcony rail was low and the man had gone over it. Bob had wheeled from the window, not hearing the shriek and *thud* that had followed his kick. He hadn't seen those teeth in Tucson—of that he was positive. One other place remained: Gila City. Dandy Bob had dressed rapidly. If he hurried, he could have McMain's company on the ride.

So it came about that McMain, the restraining order on the Limerick Girl, and Dandy Bob Roberts arrived in Gila City simultaneously.

161

From the stage stop Dandy Bob and the deputy went directly to the widow's cottage, McMain wishing to get his unpleasant business done.

They found the widow halfway tearful, halfway flattered and coquettish. She accepted service of the restraining order and told her visitors that she had already been notified.

"Mike's brother was here an' a fine big man he is," the widow announced. "Sure, he has the very look of the Fennessys about him. If him an' me could get together, there'd be no trouble at all, at all. It's the lawyers that make the trouble."

To this McMain and Bob agreed, and, at the widow's request, the deputy furnished her with the name of a reputable attorney in Tucson. "You'll have to pay him a retainer," he warned, "an' your account in Tucson is tied up."

Bob felt largely in his pocket and brought out a roll of bills, big enough to plug a fruit jar. "Here," he said, sorting through them. "I'll stake you, Missus Fennessy. There's a thousand. Pay me when you get things cleared up. You take the stage up to Tucson an' get the best lawyer you can on the job."

"If I must, I must," the widow said. "Thanks to ye, Bob. 'Tis good to have friends. Duggan's run out on me."

"Where is Duggan?" Bob demanded.

"Faith, an' I don't know." The widow turned her back, bent, and silk rustled. When she faced them again, she was empty-handed. "Duggan's no good at all, but this Fennessy man. What a beautiful, big mustache."

Bob and McMain left the widow and went on to town, parting at the hotel. McMain went in to secure a room, brushing past a large, bewhiskered gentleman who was laden with a bundle of laundry. Bob began a search for Duggan.

He did not find the gentleman. Duggan was not in the Rajah or the Mint or any of his accustomed haunts. Bob gave up and, since it was growing late, walked to his adobe at the edge of the town. The door was locked, plain evidence that Duggan was not within.

Bob left the door open to air out the single room and, lighting the lamp, took off his travel-stained clothing and cleaned up. His last few days in Tucson had been so filled as to preclude any care of his person, and now he shaved and washed himself. Then, collecting his laundry into a bundle, he tied it and put it on the bed. Dressing carefully, he cocked his black hat up on his head and, picking up the bundle, left the adobe. He would drop his laundry at Wong T'seng's, and then go on his way to supper.

With the bundle under his arm Dandy Bob strolled along through the gathering gloom. He wondered where in the world Duggan had hidden himself. Dandy Bob wanted to see Duggan. He wanted to rub it in.

IV

"DRUNKARD'S AGREEMENT"

Not knowing of Dandy Bob's return, Duggan showed up at the Mint Saloon. The old man needed liquid encouragement and he got it in the shape of three quick drinks. It appeared to Duggan that the world was tumbling down about his ears and Bob Roberts was not on hand to help him out. Following his drinks, he bought a full quart of liquor and, laden with the whiskey and his shotgun, he wandered out of the saloon.

The time was almost five in the afternoon—not that Duggan cared or noticed. He knew only that the sun was hot and he was in trouble. The old man paid no attention to where his feet took him, and, presently, he reached the desert beyond the edge of town. A paloverde beckoned and in its scanty shade Duggan sat down to drink and to think. He was three drinks down on the bottle when the Tucson stage passed by. The road was hidden from the paloverde and Duggan did not see the vehicle.

The old man's thoughts were far from cheerful. He was scared and shamed and mad, all at the same time. He realized, very fully now, that without Dandy Bob Roberts he could not succeed as justice of the peace. Somebody would stop his clock for him. Probably somebody was already planning to stop his clock. So much for item one.

On top of this was Violet Fennessy's trouble. Duggan coveted the widow's wealth, but, more than this, he was genuinely fond of Violet. His impotence to help her made him realize his smallness and his limitations.

Now, sided by the whiskey, Duggan began to feel sorry for himself. If he had not become justice of the peace, none of this would have happened. Duggan took another big drink. The sun was going down and at that unfortunate moment Henry Hinkle arrived at the paloverde.

Hinkle had ridden out to inspect a loan. He was returning to town and, seeing a man under a paloverde, stopped to investigate. He saw Duggan, he saw the bottle, and he guessed Duggan's state. A true son of Temperance, Henry could not pass by such an opportunity.

"Drunk!" he said scathingly. "My brother, don't you realize that liquor will be your downfall?"

Mistily Duggan recognized the speaker. Here in front of him was something concrete and objective. Duggan presented the shotgun. "If you'd been elected," he said thickly, "it wouldn't have happened. 'S all your fault."

Henry flinched away from the shotgun. "The liquor is at fault," he refuted. "Your own disgusting habits have led you into this sad condition."

"Ish th' only fren' I got." Duggan picked up the bottle and drank deeply but the shotgun remained alert. "Whyn't you campaign harder? What you wanna lettum elec' me for?"

"My dear, good friend," soothed Henry, "you are quite evidently laboring under a misapprehension. I tried to become justice of the peace. Indeed, I did."

"Loushy job," Duggan stated flatly. "Ge' down!"

Henry dismounted and, under the influence of the shotgun, approached.

"Sed down!" Duggan commanded. "Have a drink."

"I don't drink," said Henry.

"You *do* drink," said Duggan, extending the bottle.

Henry drank.

The Chapin & Gore took hold with authority. That drink hit Henry like a rope hose hits the end of a reata. "Take 'nother," Duggan insisted hospitably. "Pore feller. Wansh to be justish peash."

Henry took another and passed the bottle. Duggan, absolutely fair, took two drinks to catch up, and gave the bottle back. Henry killed it.

"No more liquor," Duggan stated. "Shad."

"Shad," Henry agreed.

"Go 'n' get shum," Duggan stated, and staggered to his feet. "C'm on."

Nothing loath, Henry also arose. Henry's horse had wandered off and the two men tacked across the desert. Obliquely, and with tangling feet, they arrived at Bob's adobe. Finding it open—for Dandy Bob had just left—Henry lit the lamp and with the yellow light of burning kerosene for illumination, Duggan sought and found. He had a half pint of Chapin & Gore hidden for emergencies such as this. Companionably the two seated themselves and opened the bottle.

"Shad," Duggan said once again. "You wan' justish peash. I doan wan' justish peash. I resign. You be justish."

Henry was not so far gone as Duggan, but he had gone far enough. Such generosity appealed to him. It was noble of Duggan, just plain noble, and he should be rewarded. Henry searched his pockets and brought out a paper.

"Sh'loon," said Henry. "Rajah Sh'loon. You be sh'loonkeeper . . . I'll be justish peash. Gotta pen?"

After some search and another drink, Duggan found the desired pen and a piece of blank paper. "Write out reshignation," he directed. "I'll sign. You be justish peash."

Henry, not too befuddled to write, scrawled on the paper. Duggan assayed his name and a blot. "There," he said proudly, as one who has done a good deed.

Henry was not done writing. On the back of the note Bliss Cassidy had given him, Henry Hinkle scrawled an endorsement and signed his name. "Here," he said. "Heresh sh'loon. Trade?"

They traded and thereafter killed the half pint. Henry was sleepy at this juncture, but Duggan would not hear of rest.

"Got to shelebrate," Duggan insisted. "Freedom. C'mon." He dragged the unwilling Henry to his feet, collected the shotgun, and, leading his weaving fellow, set out for town.

"Rajah Sh'loon," Henry suggested drowsily. "That'sh place."

"Sure," Duggan agreed.

V

"SHARE YOUR LIQUOR"

Dandy Bob, all unaware of what was happening in his adobe, stopped and left his laundry bundle. Wong T'seng, glad that his benefactor had returned, was already sorting wash but ceased when Bob arrived.

"Tucson no good?" Wong demanded, receiving Bob's bundle. "You come home, stay?"

"Maybe," Bob said, eyeing the laundry Wong had been sorting. "Say, that's a good-lookin' shirt, that striped one there."

Wong held up the shirt. "San Flancisco shirt," he said. "Just come."

"How do you know it's from San Francisco?" Bob demanded, his curiosity aroused.

"Laundly ma'k," Wong explained. "My cousin laundly. I wash there. See? On colleh?" He displayed a small hieroglyphic on the collar of the shirt.

"I'll take your word for it." Bob laughed. "Who brought it in?"

"Big man. Big whiskeh likes so." Wong demonstrated a sweeping mustache. "I-lish mans."

"A big Irishman with whiskers, huh?" Bob's eyes were thoughtful. "What's his name?"

"No say name. Laundly ma'k say O-halah."

"O-halah? You mean O'Hara?"

"Sure. O-Halah. Tha's what Wong say."

"And he's from San Francisco?"

"All clothes ma'k my cousin laundly. Suah. San Flancisco."

"Hmmm," said Bob Roberts, puzzled. "Well, do a good job on that wash of mine, Wong."

"Suah." Wong grinned toothily. "You fliend Wong. Do good job."

Leaving Wong to his sorting, Bob made his way to town. He looked in at the Mint and ate a leisurely supper in the Elite Restaurant. Then, still wondering about Duggan's whereabouts, he walked to the Rajah. Frank McMain was at the bar and beckoned Bob over.

"Have a drink?" the deputy invited. "This is a stinkin' job I've got, Bob. I hated to serve that order on the widow."

"Too soon after supper for a drink," Bob answered. "Who is all that down at the end of the bar, Frank?"

"You know Cassidy an' Axtell," McMain replied. "The big guy with 'em is Pat Fennessy, Mike's brother. He's the one that's caused all the ruckus."

Bob eyed the group at the bar end with interest. The big man was talking, gesturing with a small glass of whiskey while Bert Axtell and Bliss Cassidy listened. Remembering his winnings in the poker game, Bob brought out his wallet and extracted the draft and invoice he had won. Two thousand dollars was a lot of money and he meant to collect every cent of it.

Fennessy finished what he was saying and Cassidy and Axtell laughed. Gold glinted in the lamplight and Bob Roberts started.

"Dos dientes del oro." He could still hear his would-be assassin's voice.

"Axtell been up to Tucson lately?" Bob drawled.

"Sure," said McMain. "He was up there gettin' that

restrainin' order an' attachin' the widow's bank account. Damn him anyhow. An' damn that big Mick! I wish he'd stayed in Boston."

"Boston?" Roberts's question came quick and hard.

"Sure he's from Boston. Why?"

"Come on down with me, Frank," Bob Roberts ordered. "This is crooked as a dog's hind leg." In Bob Roberts's mind things had clicked together, forming a pattern.

McMain, mystified but backing Bob, followed down the bar.

Bliss Cassidy was behind the bar, the other two across it, facing him. All three turned as Bob approached and astonishment flickered across the faces of the saloon man and the lawyer. Then Cassidy scowled and Axtell grinned weakly.

"What's on your mind, Roberts?" Cassidy demanded.

"I've got a draft here," Dandy Bob replied. "It's on you an' I won it from Groome Hance up in Tucson. It amounts to two thousand, Cassidy."

"That draft will be paid," Cassidy growled. "It ain't due yet. I got some time on it."

"It *is* due," Bob said levelly. "It's a sight draft an' I want the money. A man ought to pay his debts. Ain't that right . . . O'Hara?"

The false Pat Fennessy was caught off base. "Sure," he began. "But. . . ."

"An' that cinches it!" Bob snapped. "You're no more Pat Fennessy than I am. Your name's O'Hara an' you live in San Francisco. You an' these two bastards are tryin' to rook the Widow Fennessy!"

Attention in the Rajah Saloon had centered on the group at the back end of the bar. As Dandy Bob Roberts spoke, men shifted hurriedly, those nearest the door making for it, the others diving for whatever shelter they could find.

It was just as well. With Bob's final word, both Cassidy and Axtell went for their weapons. O'Hara, befuddled and not knowing who he faced, was slower than his companions.

Bob matched Cassidy. His hand swept aside his long coattail and his draw equaled the saloon man's. In the Rajah, guns roared and bucked, the air quivering with the sound, the lamps flickering with the concussion.

Cassidy, hit hard, sank down behind the bar, and Dandy Bob turned on Axtell. The lawyer had a Derringer, a snubnosed, murderous weapon. His first shot had torn the broadcloth of Dandy Bob's coat for Bert Axtell had tried for the head. Now, realizing his mistake, he was aiming lower, but he did not fire the Derringer's second barrel.

A man got only one chance at Bob Roberts, and he had to make good that single opportunity. The Derringer dropped from Axtell's nerveless fingers, and, following the weapon, Bert Axtell crumpled and went down.

Bob Roberts, feet widespread and braced, shoved his gun almost into O'Hara's face. O'Hara let go his drawn pistol and lifted his hands shoulder high.

"Don't!" he quavered. "Don't ye, now!"

Frank McMain, taken utterly by surprise, had his gun out and leveled, but, when O'Hara quit, the deputy lowered his weapon. He took a quick step forward, a question on his lips, but for the instant it was not spoken.

"That's it," Dandy Bob said, wheeling slowly. "I was right. They framed the Widow Fennessy and Bert Axtell hired a man in Tucson to kill me."

With the shooting over, the men in the saloon came from their sanctuaries and gathered around. Cassidy and Bert Axtell were dead, for Bob had been shooting for keeps. McMain, taking charge by right of authority, demanded an explanation, and, to the deputy and the listening crowd, Bob Roberts gave it.

"It's plain enough, Frank. Axtell an' Cassidy rigged this up. That big guy ain't Pat Fennessy, at all. Ask him who he is. Make him tell you."

McMain turned on the sweating O'Hara.

Under pressure, O'Hara disclosed his identity and told his story. He had been hired by Bliss Cassidy and brought in from San Francisco to impersonate Mike Fennessy's brother. The letters he had were forged. Axtell and Cassidy intended to get the Limerick Girl from the Widow Fennessy. O'Hara blurted it all out, mingling his story with a claim of innocence. He had only been a dupe, O'Hara declared, an innocent victim.

Scowling faces all about said that the crowd did not believe O'Hara.

Amidst all the confusion, Doc Speers, summoned from his home, arrived and began an examination of the bodies.

Frank McMain stepped back. "You were right, Bob," he stated, "but how you figured it I'll never know. What put you on to 'em?"

"A pair of gold teeth an' some dirty shirts," Bob answered. "Wong's cousin runs a laundry in San Francisco an' O'Hara happened to take his clothes there. Wong knew the laundry mark. You'd better get O'Hara in jail with a guard. This crowd is gettin' ugly. I wonder where Duggan is."

As though in answer to the question, Old Man Duggan and Henry Hinkle, arm in arm, came through the Rajah's door. Both were disheveled, both obviously drunk, and Hinkle was carrying Duggan's shotgun.

The two men paused in the doorway and Duggan eyed the crowd. " 'S my sh'loon," he announced to the world at large. "Drinksh for the crowd, bartender!"

"You're drunk," Dandy Bob accused, leaving McMain and pushing through to the pair in the doorway. "You're drunk, Duggan. You're justice of the peace an' we got a prisoner for your jail."

"*He'sh* justish peash!" Duggan jerked his head toward Henry Hinkle. "I reshined."

Henry blinked his eyes. The shotgun rested on his arm, both hammers cocked. " 'S right." Henry nodded agreement. "He's sh'loon man . . . I'm justish peash. Sh'loon's wicked. Goin' close 'em up."

"Let down the hammers on that gun!" McMain commanded, approaching warily. "You'll kill somebody. What in the hell is this, anyway, Bob?"

"Damn if I know," Dandy Bob answered. "I don't *sabe*. . . ."

The sentence was never finished. O'Hara, attention distracted from him by Duggan and Hinkle's entrance, made his break. O'Hara was in a tight and knew it. He had eased around the crowd, almost to the door, and, as Bob spoke, he ran. Out through the door he went, intent on escape. He almost made it.

But not quite. Henry Hinkle was a law-abiding citizen and his eyes had seen the star McMain wore. McMain had said to let down the shotgun hammers and Henry lowered them by pulling both triggers. The shotgun roared and out in the street O'Hara squalled his hurt. Henry was knocked down by the blast and McMain stepped on him as he dashed after the escaping prisoner.

The crowd followed McMain, the Rajah emptying as if by magic. Everybody left—everybody but Bob Roberts, Old Man Duggan, and Henry Hinkle. Henry lay where he had fallen, and Old Man Duggan, with a howl of fright, threw both arms around Bob Roberts's neck and climbed aboard.

Bob fought the old man off and, finally getting clear,

looked all about. Henry slept peacefully, still clutching the shotgun. Duggan trembled in Bob's grasp. From the street came diminishing sounds, shouts, and shots. Dandy Bob Roberts, still holding Duggan, took a long step, closed the Rajah's door, and turned the key. Then, dragging the old man, he headed for a chair.

"Now," snarled Dandy Bob, "I'm goin' to get to the bottom of this."

It took some time, it took some questioning, it took patience. There were interruptions. Bob had to open the door and let in men to remove the bodies of Axtell and Cassidy. He had to shake Henry Hinkle awake, search Henry's pockets, and listen to some talk so thick that it was almost indecipherable.

An even hour after O'Hara had made his break, Bob answered a knock on the Rajah's door and let in Frank McMain. The deputy looked worn. He picked up a glass of whiskey from the bar, drank it, and stared at Dandy Bob.

"Well," McMain said, "O'Hara's in jail. Two buckshot got him in the seat of the pants an' he couldn't run fast enough. I got Frazee an' Watson an' some more guardin' him so he won't be lynched."

Bob nodded soberly. "Come back here, Frank," he directed, and led the way to a table.

Old Man Duggan and Henry Hinkle, both asleep and snoring gently, were sprawled on the table. Before them lay certain documents. Bob selected one and passed it to McMain.

"What do you think of that?" Bob asked.

McMain read, looked up, and grinned broadly. "It looks like Duggan resigned, all right," he said. "The writin' ain't good but I can read it."

"Yeah," Bob agreed. "He resigned. Look at this."

McMain examined a second paper. "Why, this is a note," he announced, "made out by Cassidy to Hinkle with a mortgage in the Rajah attached. Hinkle's endorsed it over to Duggan."

"An' that means," said Dandy Bob Roberts, "that Duggan owns the Rajah, don't it? Cassidy's dead."

McMain nodded slowly.

"Then, where," said Dandy Bob, "do I come in? I've got a sight draft for two thousand dollars an' an invoice for the liquor Hance sold Cassidy. How do I collect, and who do I collect it from?"

"From the saloon," McMain replied. "You an' Duggan are partners, Bob. You own the Rajah between you."

"That's what I thought," Dandy Bob Roberts said resignedly, and sat down heavily.

Silence fell in the Rajah Saloon. Frank McMain broke it. "What's the matter, Bob?" he demanded. "You ain't lettin' it get you down, are you? Shucks, you had to shoot. Axtell an' Cassidy had it comin'. You won't have no trouble about them. An' the widow's all right. That restrainin' order an' the attachment on her bank account will be lifted off just as soon as I get back to Tucson. What's the matter, Bob?"

"It ain't that." Dandy Bob made a small and weary gesture. "That ain't what bothers me."

"Then what?" McMain put his hand on Bob's shoulder.

"It's Duggan," Bob answered. "Old Man Duggan. That's what bothers me. Him an' me are partners in this saloon, an' how am I goin' to keep him from drinkin' up the profits?"

Duggan Trouble
at Salado Wash

I

"DUGGAN'S DUMBBELL"

As half owner of the Rajah Saloon, Dandy Bob Roberts discovered he occupied a definite place in Gila City's social structure. The town counted on him to serve good liquor in full measure, to keep his gambling games honest, to watch his bartenders and see they didn't shortchange drunks, and to be responsible for Old Man Duggan. All that was foreign to Bob's habits of thought and action. He had spent his life in figuring angles and taking advantage of the same, so honesty came hard. It was harder still to look after Duggan. That amiable drunkard considered the whole world legitimate prey, and his whiskey-soaked brain could conjure up ideas that appalled even Dandy Bob. Still, Bob Roberts tried. Credit must be given him; he tried.

"Look here, Duggan," Bob ordered after they had operated the Rajah for a month. "We own this joint an' we've got to keep it respectable. A saloonkeeper can't get a man drunk an' then roll him in the alley. Give me that blackjack you've been carryin'."

Duggan searched his partner's face and saw that Dandy Bob meant what he said. In the past, the two had committed various acts of chicanery and the old man could hardly believe his ears. To have Dandy Bob suddenly turn pure was no more surprising than to find Satan backstopping for the Angel Gabriel. Hastily, to settle his nerves, Duggan took a big drink of Chapin & Gore.

"But Bob . . . ," he expostulated.

"Give it to me or I'll tell the Widow Fennessy," Bob commanded sternly.

Violet Fennessy—the Widow Fennessy—was owner of the Limerick Girl silver mine and Duggan's affianced. To Duggan she represented life without labor—and he was afraid of losing her. At the moment Duggan was on probation with the widow, and Dandy Bob could have thought of no more potent threat. Reluctantly the old man passed over the blackjack.

"How long are we goin' to do this lily-white act?" Duggan grumbled as Dandy Bob pocketed the weapon. "I'm gettin' tired of goin' around with my face all screwed up like I was a preacher. What's the matter with you, Bob? You ain't yourself no more."

This was true, although Roberts failed to realize it. One month of rectitude, of being a respectable citizen, had done things to Bob. He always had commanded a certain prestige—his sartorial splendor and his ability with a .45 Colt insured him that—but now, as he conducted his business along strictly legitimate lines, he began to enter a different stage. Although Bob was entirely unaware of it, the solid and substantial citizens of his bailiwick regarded him and his opinions with respect.

"I'm just as much myself as I ever was," he assured Duggan. "An' we're goin' to be honest until the right deal comes along. I ain't goin' to throw the Rajah away for peanuts, but when the chance comes for a real killin', I'll take it. I think we might make a nice profit."

Bob Roberts thought that this was so. He believed what he said. Duggan also believed it and was satisfied. Neither of them realized that habit is a subtle thing and that customs of honesty may become ingrained.

So, beginning with the acquisition of the Rajah Saloon,

Dandy Bob Roberts walked the path of rectitude and responsibility, with Duggan, in a manner of speaking, stalking in his shadow. Gila City watched, skeptically at first, and then accepted the change. The attitude of Gila City was expressed by tough old Jim Conway, owner of the 77 brand.

"Bob Roberts," said Conway, in from his ranch and foregathered with solid citizens in the Rajah, "has done changed his spots. He used to be a wild one. Time was when I figured he maybe stole a few cattle from me, but maybe I was wrong. He's makin' a go of this saloon an' he's holdin' Ol' Man Duggan in line. Looks like he turned into a pretty good man."

Solemn nods agreed with Conway. Mentally the group recapitulated those episodes in which Bob Roberts had played a part: the shooting scrapes with Tom Harmes and Bliss Cassidy, the expedition to Freedom Hill in which, despite Apaches, Bob and Duggan had delivered the Christmas mail, the discovery of the lost vein in the Limerick Girl and the restoration of the mine to Violet Fennessy. All those things Bob Roberts had done, albeit unwillingly and unwittingly.

"Yeah," Frazee, the postmaster, seconded Conway, "Bob's all right. You know, he might not be a bad man to run for mayor next fall."

Again the solemn nods ran around the circle. So, six months after his acquisition of the Rajah, Bob Roberts was respected, and not alone for his ability to shoot. This might have continued indefinitely except for Old Man Duggan. Old Man Duggan believed that Bob was only waiting for a killing, and honesty palled upon him. He forced the issue.

There were two freighting outfits in Gila City, each with its own wagon yard. One of these was operated in conjunction with the Star Livery barn, which was also the stage stop.

The other was owned by Ladd Quentin and Wilsey Lea. Quentin and Lea had established their business shortly after Bob and Duggan acquired the Rajah Saloon. Quentin was as tall as Dandy Bob and, like Bob, affected the clothing of a gambler—broadcloth coat, broad black hat, immaculate linen, and shiny boots. From a distance the similarity between the two was striking, and it was only at close range that differences could be noted.

Wilsey Lea was a small, hard-bitten man who paid little attention to dress. His eyes were small, blue, and mean, but his voice was low and soft. Gila City sized Wilsey Lea up as a hardcase, his partner, also.

Quentin and Lea did custom hauling. They pulled freight to the mines, they hauled from Tucson, they took the small jobs, the leftovers—and they made a living. Both were gamblers, shrewd players at poker, faro, and monte, and both were horsemen.

Old Man Duggan also fancied himself as a connoisseur of horseflesh. Among the other appurtenances of Bliss Cassidy, inherited with the Rajah Saloon, was a horse known as Dumbbell. Dumbbell showed breeding and a turn of speed. Dumbbell had beaten everything on four legs around Gila City. Duggan boasted and bragged about Dumbbell as fluently as he lied concerning his own prowess against the Apaches. Naturally Wilsey Lea and Ladd Quentin heard and listened to these lies.

In the Lea and Quentin stable was a hammerheaded, rawboned roan horse, and, prior to their advent in Gila City, the roan had made a living for the partners. Quentin and Lea foregathered and talked things over.

"Yeah," Ladd Quentin said at the end of the consultation, "but not while Bob Roberts is in town. He'd get wise. Wait till he pulls out an' then we'll spring it." So the partners bided their time.

Summer drew to a close and fall approached. The Widow Fennessy took Duggan off the probation list and set a date for the wedding. Dandy Bob Roberts decided to visit Tucson and see the liquor wholesalers. He needed a bust, needed relief from the steady pattern of rectitude. The widow decided that she, too, would visit the metropolis and order her wedding finery. Bob and the widow departed for the Old Pueblo on the stage. Wilsey Lea and Ladd Quentin saw them go and exchanged significant glances.

Tucson received her visitors with aplomb and pleasure. The widow foregathered with the town's most fashionable dressmaker. Bob sought his old companions. Tucson was familiar to him; twice a year he visited the place. His friends greeted him joyously, but it was different from former occasions. Whereas, before, he had been a gambler, a sharp-shooter in town for a good time, now he was a respected businessman whose opinions and counsel were sought. There was a constraint upon him, and, unbelievably, he found this pleasant. He drank a little and he played a little poker but it was for amusement only.

On his fourth day in town he sat into a game with Bert Sughman, down from Prescott and an old acquaintance. Talk around the table was desultory and, in some manner, the names of Quentin and Lea were mentioned. Sughman, who was shuffling the deck, paused in his endeavor and looked up.

"Them two," Sughman said. "A little man that looks like a hardcase an' a big man that dresses like a gambler? I know 'em." He passed the deck for a cut, retrieved it, and began the deal.

"They were in Prescott a year ago," Sughman said, "an' they took the camp. Cabbaged on to all the loose cash the boys had. Done it with a horse." He continued, describing the operations of Lea and Quentin in Prescott, and, as he talked, a faint, uneasy feeling began to grow in the pit of Bob Roberts's belly.

"It was the old get-drunk-an'-bet business," Sughman said. "Lea acted like he was full an' bragged about this roan. The roan didn't look like he could run a stroke. They tolled us on, let us win a race, an' then, when the real money was bet, that roan horse just breezed in. We asked for it, but it come hard. Them two are smooth operators."

Sughman picked up his cards and scanned them. Bob Roberts, the faint feeling growing, folded his hand and pushed it to the center of the table. "Cash me in," he requested. "I just thought of somethin'."

The Widow Fennessy was not nearly done with her dressmaking, so Bob returned to Gila City alone. He rode the top of the stage because progress seemed swifter from that vantage point. Twice during the trip, signal smokes were seen from the hills, thin pillars of rising vapor, now white, now black. Driver and guard spoke feelingly of these, forecasting trouble from Apaches, but Bob hardly heard their comments. When he reached Gila City, the town appeared deserted; only the hostlers were on hand to meet the stage.

"Where is everybody?" Bob demanded.

"Out on the flat north of town," a hostler answered. "Horse race out there."

Bob waited for no more. He left his grip at the stage stop and hurried.

Gila City was assembled on the flat; all the town was there. Bob pushed through the crowd, searching for Old Man Duggan. He found him, together with Watson, the assayer, Frazee, Stevens of the Holy Ghost Mine, and Ladd Quentin.

Duggan was jubilant. "Jest in time, Bob," the old man chortled. "In another ten minutes you're goin' to be a wealthy man." Duggan's breath was heavy with Chapin & Gore perfume.

"What's the score?" Bob asked. He spoke to Duggan but his eyes were on Quentin.

Quentin smiled thinly. "Your pardner matched a race with Lea an' me," he said easily. "Runnin' your Dumbbell horse against a nag of ours. We got a little bet on it."

Watson said: "They want me to hold stakes, Bob. Duggan, here, wants to bet the Rajah against Quentin and Lea's wagon yard. I didn't know. . . ."

"That's the bet," Quentin interposed smoothly. "It ain't a question of wantin' to make it. It's already been made. Ain't that right, Frazee?"

Jim Frazee nodded reluctantly. "I was in the Rajah when Duggan made it," he said. "But look here. Duggan only owns half the saloon. If Bob don't want to bet his half. . . ."

"Of course, if Roberts wants to back out," Quentin interrupted, "I won't say a word." There was scorn and a question in his voice. Men had gathered around and were listening.

Duggan opened his mouth to speak, but closed it again as Bob made answer. "Who have you got to ride Dumbbell?" he asked.

"Apolonius García," Duggan answered. "Look-it here, Bob. I figure that. . . ."

"I know how you figure," Bob snapped. His eyes met Quentin's. A dead game sport, Bob Roberts. "All right, Quentin. Run your race. I'll back my pardner's bet."

Quentin grinned thinly, for he was over the hump. Bob Roberts was a gambling man who would not welch. "Here's a deed to the wagon yard," Quentin said, and pushed a paper at Watson.

"I got a deed to the Rajah made out," Duggan crowed. "I've signed it. You sign it, Bob."

"Give it here," said Bob Roberts, "an' give me a pencil." He scrawled his name below Duggan's and passed the deed to Watson. "Now," he continued grimly, "let's run the race."

Preliminaries were attended to, a starter selected, judges picked. Bob and Duggan put Apolonius up on Dumbbell. Wilsey Lea, stripped down to shirt and trousers, rode the roan. Duggan chattered blithely, certain of victory. Bob was grimly silent. Not until the horses lined up did the old man notice his partner's lack of enthusiasm.

"What's the matter, Bob?" Duggan demanded. "Look-it. I spent all the time you was gone linin' this thing up. Them fellers ain't got a chance. Why, Dumbbell c'n outrun his shadder, you know that! That roan horse. . . ."

"Will beat Dumbbell thirty feet!" Bob snapped. "The roan's a ringer!"

Duggan's eyes widened with astonishment. "Then why'd you bet?" he demanded. "Why didn't you back out?"

"An' welch?" Dandy Bob snarled. "Not me!"

Bystanders stared curiously, then talk ceased abruptly as a shot sounded. The two horses, bay and roan, came pounding down the course. Along the track each man leaned forward. The bay had a lead, a trifling lead. The bay horse was ahead. The bay horse.

The roan stretched his hammerhead. Wilsey Lea lay along the roan's neck and his whip fell. The roan's belly flattened to the ground. Up to the bay, even with the bay, ahead of the bay. The roan horse fairly flew. Now there was a gap between the horses. They thundered across the finish.

Old Man Duggan straightened up, his face as gray as his beard. He found his voice. "Bob," he gasped, "we're paupers!"

II

"GUN CHORE FOR A PAUPER"

One week after the race Dandy Bob Roberts sat in his adobe at the edge of Gila City and looked at Old Man Duggan. Duggan snored on a bed. Certain of Bob's friends had suggested that he kill the old man, and Bob had been tempted. Duggan himself had suggested that Bob kill Quentin and Lea. He had also suggested various other enterprises, ranging from stealing cattle to holding up the stage. Bob looked at Old Man Duggan and wondered why he had not taken the suggestions. Here he was, right back in the position he had occupied before owning the Rajah, and he wasn't stirring a hand. He had played some poker, honestly, and won a little money, but then he had always been honest at poker. He had listened to Duggan's suggestions—and had shaken his head.

He couldn't steal cattle, not when old Jim Conway had come around and gruffly suggested that, in case Bob needed a little money, he, Conway, had some cash to spare. He couldn't high-grade ore from the Holy Ghost. Not when Stevens, the manager, had diffidently offered Bob a job "just to tide him over until something came up." He couldn't put his heart into holding up a stage, not when the division manager had offered him a job as shotgun guard. All the common aspects of dishonesty were closed to Dandy Bob Roberts. He looked at Duggan and scowled.

Duggan snored peacefully. For one day Duggan had been filled with wild self-recrimination, also with Chapin & Gore.

At the end of that time the old man bounced back with a plan to steal the roan and use the horse to make money. On the second day the Widow Fennessy had returned to Gila City, heard the news, and summoned Bob into executive council. Duggan was back on the blacklist, in the doghouse as usual, but Violet Fennessy had placed the whole Limerick Girl at Bob's disposal. Dandy Bob shuddered slightly. The Widow Fennessy wanted to get married. She would take Old Man Duggan if she could get nothing better, but she was in the market and looking around. Bob knew that he was on her shopping list. Violet and Duggan, he thought, would make an ideal pair and he wished that they were safely married. He also wished that the old, familiar twist would come to him. Here he was, practically broke, and he couldn't figure an angle. Not a solitary thing. He picked up his hat, arose, adjusted gun and belt under the tails of his Prince Albert, and walked out. It was noon and time to eat.

Lunch was postponed. Gila City boiled with excitement and Bob joined the crowd at the stage station. The stage had just come in, filled with bullet holes and plentifully sprinkled with iron arrow points. The Apaches were out. Geronimo was raiding along the border.

Arizona Territory knew all about Apaches, knowledge gained the hard way. Apaches were a daily hazard, like falling into mine shafts or being thrown by a broncho, but this was no ordinary, everyday affair, as it developed. In the days that followed, Gila City, as well as the rest of Arizona, learned that fact. The Tonto tribe was off the reservation, the Mimbrés and Chiricahuas were raiding; the whole Apache nation was on the warpath. From Lordsburg in New Mexico to Yuma on the river, men walked warily and waited for the Army to get busy.

The Army got busy. From Bowie and Grant and all the

posts located for just such contingencies, the troops moved out, and with the troops moved Pima scouts and others from the White Mountain Apaches, glad to take government rations and pay while playing the old game of war. They moved, and moved again, but it was like chasing a will-o'-the-wisp. Apaches disappeared into Mexico where they rested and recruited before returning to the fray. Weary cavalrymen rode and swore and rode again, and even their wily foe disappeared when contact was made. Ruined ranches smoked in Sulphur Springs Valley, at Dos Cabezas and Tres Hermanas. Lonely prospectors awoke to the war whoop and died before their own shrieks sounded. The stage ran only at intervals, and then with an escort. But the stage brought mail and rumor.

Rumor. An ugly thing. A prospector, hard wounded, had reached Tucson, and, before he died, he told a story of new repeating rifles in the hands of his attackers. A ranchman reached Prescott with the same tale. Someone, someone in Arizona or New Mexico Territory, was doing business with the savages. Somewhere, in Tucson or Lordsburg, in Nogales or Phoenix or maybe Gila City, were men—no, not men, two-legged vultures—to whom a dollar loomed bigger than human life. Arizona Territory cursed. If we get our hands on them, it's a rope, that's all. A rope! But who could it be? You, maybe? Or you? Or you? Arizona forted up, moved only when it had to move, and watched.

In Gila City, disaster struck. A wagon train out from Tucson, belonging to the Gila City Star Livery, was jumped on Dixon Flat. The wagons, loaded with food, liquor, and other essentials, were looted and burned.

In Gila City, Tom Grady who owned the Mint Saloon, and Adolf Britenback of the Tivoli, and Delfino Dominguez,

189

who operated the *cantina,* came to call upon Dandy Bob Roberts.

"We got a little proposition to make to you, Bob," said Grady, spokesman for the trio. "We talked it over amongst us an' we got a job. We think you can do it."

Dandy Bob sat on the edge of his bed. His callers occupied chairs. "Go ahead," Bob directed.

"We're runnin' out of liquor," Grady stated. "I'm down to two barrels an' some bottle stuff. Adolf ain't no better off, an' all Fino's got left is straight mescal. We want you to bring us some liquor from Tucson."

"What about Quentin an' Lea's outfit?" Bob asked. "They been makin' trips."

Grady shook his head. "They won't haul for us," he answered. "I talked to Quentin. He says there's no point in him furnishin' liquor to competitors. He says when we run out an' want a drink, we can buy it at the Rajah."

Bob nodded understanding. Quentin was a sharp one, all right, and so was Lea.

"So we want you to go to Tucson an' bring out two loads." Grady consulted the others with his eyes and Adolf and Delfino nodded agreement. "We got what we need figured out. We trust you . . . an' you're known in Tucson. You slide up there, just however you can, buy mules an' wagons an' hire men, an' we'll give you an order on the wholesale house. You bring the liquor back."

"Why me?" Bob drawled. "Why not one of you?"

"Because," Grady said frankly, "you're a fightin' man. We ain't."

There was a long silence while Bob thought. "What do I get?" he asked.

"We thought maybe the wagons an' mules," Grady answered. "You'd be set up in the freightin' business, then."

Again silence. Then: "Get your letters written an' the money together," Bob Roberts directed. "I'll pull out tonight. An' keep it quiet. No need to talk."

"We won't talk," Grady promised, "an' we'll have everything ready. We're glad you're goin', Bob."

The three saloonkeepers left, and Dandy Bob sat on his bed, studying the empty doorway. Presently he got up and began his preparations, taking his rifle from the rack by the door and carrying it, with rod and oil and patches, to the table. While he was engaged upon the gun, Old Man Duggan came in.

"Bunch of soldiers just hit town," Duggan announced. "Camped down below the creek. They're plumb wore out. Them horses are drawed up till they're snipe-gutted. I seen. . . . What you doin', Bob?"

"Cleaning my gun," Bob answered.

"Yeah, I can see that. I seen that lieutenant that bosses the soldiers, an' talked to him. Tol' him if he really wanted to git him some 'Paches, I'd take him out an' show him how to do it."

"Yeah?" Bob squinted through the rifle barrel, lowered the piece, and closed the action.

"Yeah. Say, Bob, you got any money? I'm broke."

Bob Roberts drew three silver dollars from his pocket.

"Jus' a loan," Duggan said automatically, and took the money. "I'm goin' back downtown. So long, Bob. See you later." Duggan departed.

Dandy Bob, his preparations complete, left the adobe. In the Mint Saloon he took a drink and then foregathered with Tom Grady. Money and a letter passed between them, Bob pocketing them both. He ate supper at the Elite, bowed and spoke to the Widow Fennessy on the street, and returned to his adobe through the gathering dusk.

★ ★ ★ ★ ★

Down in the Rajah Saloon, with Ladd Quentin standing by, Old Man Duggan waved a whiskey glass, hiccoughed slightly, and held forth.

" 'Paches? Why, say, I was fightin' 'Paches before you was out of three-cornered pants. Why, me an' my pardner, Bob Roberts, don't think no more of fightin' 'Paches than we do of takin' a drink."

Quentin nodded to the bartender, who replenished Duggan's glass. "Tell us about the time you and Roberts took the mail to Freedom Hill," Quentin directed, winking at the bystanders. "How many Apaches were in that bunch, Duggan? Fifty?"

"Fifty!" Duggan glared around the sober-faced circle. "They was a hundred anyhow! Aw right, I'll tell you. Me an' Bob. . . ."

III

"OLD MAN DUGGAN RIDES"

In the morning Duggan wakened with a familiar headache. He groped for a bottle, found none, and sat up in bed. He was, he saw, in Bob Roberts's adobe house, which was as it should have been, but he had no recollection of coming home. This did not trouble him for he seldom remembered coming home. What did bother him was the empty bed across the room. Bob was gone. Duggan got up, made a sketchy toilet, searched for a bottle, and failed to find one. There was still a silver dollar remaining in his pocket, enough for one drink and breakfast, or for two drinks. Duggan hastened toward town.

In the Mint Saloon he took two drinks and sought to promote another. Grady was not at his place of business and the bartender was adamant. Duggan left the saloon. On the street, halfway between the Mint and the Rajah, he encountered Violet Fennessy. Although not exactly in the widow's good graces, Duggan stopped. He knew Violet would not give him drinking money, but she might be wheedled into a meal if Duggan worked it right. He commented on the widow's gown and offered to carry her basket to the store, and Violet Fennessy unbent a trifle.

Duggan was in possession of the basket when Tom Grady arrived.

" 'Mornin', Missus Fennessy," Grady greeted. Then, to Duggan: "Did Bob get away all right?"

"He ain't home," Duggan answered. "What do you mean

. . . get away? Where's Bob goin'?"

"I thought he might have told you," Grady said. "Bob's gone to Tucson to bring back some liquor for Dolf an' Delfino an' me. If he ain't at the house, he must've pulled out last night." Grady walked on to the Mint, and Duggan and the Widow Fennessy entered the Bon Ton store, where the basket was filled.

Back at the widow's cottage, Duggan unloaded the basket on the kitchen table while Violet made coffee. There was gingerbread, a weakness of Duggan's, and he ate and drank. The widow was moody and quiet.

"What's the matter, Vi'let?" Duggan inquired.

"I'm worried about Bob," the widow answered. "Goin' to Tucson all alone with all them Apaches rampagin' an' lootin' over the country. I don't like it."

"Bob should've took me with him," Duggan affirmed. "Him an' me c'n whup any bunch of 'Paches in the country." An idea struck his fertile mind. "If I jest had some money to buy ca'tridges, I'd ketch up to him. If I had ten dollars, I'd sure go an' ketch up."

The widow considered this statement, suddenly turned her back, and, with a rustling of petticoats, made a withdrawal from the bank. "Here," she said, turning. "Here's ten dollars. You get your gun an' go find Bob." The widow had a weakness for Roberts and, of all Gila City, she alone placed some small confidence in Aloysius Duggan.

Duggan took the money, gulped the last of the gingerbread and coffee, and started for the door.

"An' if I hear that you drunk up that money," the widow called after him, "you'll wish you'd found the Apaches!"

To give Duggan credit, he had, when he left the Fennessy cottage, some small idea of going to seek Bob Roberts. Duggan, as nearly as he was fond of anyone, was fond of Bob.

He carried this idea to the extent of saddling a horse and securing his shotgun, but, after that, determination failed. The horse, shotgun looped to the saddle, was tied to the Mint hitch rail, and Duggan went in. He bought a pint, bought another in case the first would not suffice for a long trip, and then, hating to open the pints, bought several drinks. Some two hours later, Jim Frazee, entering the Mint, saw Duggan at the bar.

"I saw the Widow Fennessy down the street," Frazee announced. "She's lookin' for you, Duggan."

"Good God!" Duggan paused not upon the order of his going. He hastened from the Mint Saloon. The horse was still at the hitch rail, and, with some hazy recollection that he was to ride somewhere, Duggan took the horse's reins and mounted. The pints *clinked* companionably in his pocket. Town, with Violet Fennessy looking for him, was not safe. Duggan headed out.

An hour and half a pint later Duggan reached the seclusion of a cutbank. The bank offered shade and a resting spot. Duggan accepted both. He sat in the shade, holding his bridle reins, and finished the pint, trying, as he drank, to recall where he was supposed to go. Violet had given him some money for a specific purpose but what that purpose was he could not remember. He did know that Violet would be angry. Gila City was no safe place with the widow on the warpath. Duggan wavered to his feet and mounted. In the saddle he could look over the cutbank, and did so. Horror struck him.

There, not a hundred yards away, rode a little band of Apaches, gaunt, bronzed, be-turbaned men on worn ponies. Duggan voiced one shrill yelp of fright and started from there. His heels dug into his horse's ribs and he lashed wildly with the reins. The horse, headed toward Gila City, started home. Duggan clung to his saddle horn and rode.

Whoops sounded behind. Duggan took one frightened look over his shoulder, clung all the tighter, and closed his eyes to blot out the nemesis that pursued him. All the whiskey scared out of him, he clattered down the wash, expecting, with every moment, a bullet or an arrow in the back.

Duggan's horse checked, then urged ahead by flailing heels, went on, only to check again. The animal stopped. Unwillingly Duggan opened his eyes. There were horses all about him, and a pair of hard blue eyes stared up at him. A harsh voice rasped: "What's the idea of ridin' into the picket line? You drunk?"

Old Man Duggan almost fainted with relief. He had reached the cavalry camp.

" 'Paches!" Duggan gasped. "They jumped me. I kilt two of 'em an. . . ."

The cavalryman began to laugh. All about, harsh laughter sounded. Duggan straightened. Lean, brown, be-turbaned men were riding up, broad grins on their faces.

"Them boys?" the cavalryman said. "Are them the Apaches that jumped you? Them are our scouts."

Duggan gasped like a landed fish. The brown-turbaned men were dismounting and gathering around. The cavalry lieutenant pushed through the circle and spoke abruptly.

"What is this civilian doing here, Sergeant? Get him out of here!"

"Oh, Lawd," gasped Old Man Duggan, "lemme git out. Lemme go home an' die!"

"Git, then!" The sergeant released Duggan's bridle. " 'G'wan an' git out."

Duggan's horse moved. Behind Duggan, laughter welled up. Duggan took one hasty look toward the houses and streets of Gila City. Men were riding out from town. Duggan kicked his horse in the ribs and rode.

He rode a circle, well outside the town. The horse was lathered from its run and wanted to stop. Duggan kept going. He completed the arc of his ride and, head hanging, reached the adobe house. He let the horse stand. Duggan, like a sheep-killing dog caught in the act, slunk in the adobe and sat down on his bed. The pint *clinked* in his pocket, and automatically he removed it, opened it, and took a drink. He stared at the vacant door. The drink did not help and the door told him nothing.

Clearly now he recalled his vainglorious boasting, remembered the money Violet had given him, remembered his mission and why he had saddled and ridden out. He remembered his fright and his ride and the laughter that had followed him.

Two of Duggan's Mexican neighbors passed the door and looked in curiously. Duggan winced. He knew what lay in store for him, knew that by now the story was circulating in Gila City.

Duggan could not face it. This was a thing he could not lie down or live down. There, in Bob Roberts's adobe, iron entered Old Man Duggan's soul, the iron of fear. Not fear of physical hurt or of death, but fear of scorn. Old Man Duggan got up. There was just one thing for him to do, one thing and one thing only—get out of Gila City and stay out. That was the answer.

The horse was still outside, standing on a rein. Freeing that rein, Duggan put both reins up and mounted. He rode northeast. Behind him, the autumn sun in its circle began to slide down toward the hills. Duggan rode on. The horse, weary from the chase, developed a slight limp. Duggan did not heed. The limp increased, grew greater, and presently the horse quit—quit stone cold, refusing to move.

Old Man Duggan roused from his lethargy. He tried to make the horse go on and could not. Dismounting, he tried to lead. The horse hung back. Old Man Duggan swore. He took the shotgun from the saddle, took the saddle and dumped it by a paloverde, stripped off the bridle, and turned the horse loose. He looked back the way he had come, grunted, and stepped resolutely out. Again he went northeast. He was alone and he had a long way to go. He would keep walking. Up in New Mexico, around Red River and E-town there was gold. Duggan had never been there, but he was going. Nobody would know him in E-town. Not a soul. Duggan trudged along.

Before dark he reached a tank, a little pool of water. A jack rabbit hopped out and ran, and the shotgun boomed. The rabbit fell and Duggan hastened forward. Dry mesquite made a fire and the rabbit made a meal. Duggan camped by the tank that night.

In the morning he moved on. He knew the country, knew the scant water holes, and he had laid out his course. Also, he had changed his plans. Not E-town, but Silver City was now his destination. He walked that day, leaving the remnants of the pint alone, sweating the whiskey out of him. That night he camped by the Santa Cruz, below Tucson.

The third day found Duggan still traveling, but in sorry shape. His shoes were cut to bits by the rocks. His legs were tired. At noon Old Man Duggan reached the end of his string. He just didn't give a good damn. Still he plodded ahead. He did not hear the horses coming, did not hear the voices. Not until hands seized him did he lift his head. He was surrounded by grinning brown faces. A savage poked him in the belly with a lance. Hands wrenched away the shotgun, hands searched him. Voices jabbered. Old Man Duggan was thrust toward a horse, a sorry, ewe-necked nag. Mechanically, using the last of his strength, he mounted. His feet were lashed under the horse's belly. Again voices jabbered and then there was motion. Only the thongs that bound him held Old Man Duggan to the wooden saddle.

Presently the motion ceased. Duggan's feet were released and he was pulled down. Water, dirty and stinking, sloshed on his face and he drank, recovering a little strength. He saw a tiny fire, the faces of his captors now in bold relief, now in shadow, lighted by the flames. Duggan grunted, squirmed once, and slept, and around the fire his immediate future was decided. Duggan didn't know or care.

There was debate about the fire. This group was part of Oso Rojo's band of Apaches, recently returned from old Mexico and anxious to join their fellows. They were young bucks without reputation, and the debate concerned just that. Duggan had only one scalp and just one man could claim it; therefore, each buck was jealous of the other. The debate waxed furiously and finally a compromise was reached. To give due honor and glory to all, they would take Duggan with them, keeping him alive until such a time as they rejoined the main party. Then all could see that a captive had been taken, and all could enjoy the final torture. Old Man Duggan snored.

Sleep restored him somewhat, and in the morning there was further restoration. In order that their captive might have strength to entertain them, the Apaches fed Duggan, giving him jerky made from horsemeat, and water to drink. They mounted him on the ewe-necked horse again, tying both hands and feet. The horse was a bay mare, long-backed, long-coupled, the sorriest appearing nag of all the ponies, but taller than most. A buck led the bay mare and the others clustered around. They traveled west, moving like shadows through the country. Long before noon they had crossed the Santa Cruz and still rode west. Up ahead of Duggan, the leaders stopped. There was excited chatter. Duggan's captor, the buck that led the bay mare, joined the others. Duggan, from the height of the mare's back, could see the object of their attention.

Down below on the flats were slowly moving wagons. Away to the east was a little dust cloud. Around Duggan the savage voices chattered.

Old Man Duggan's little piggy eyes were keen. Old Man Duggan was not worth a damn. He was a coward, a liar, a cheat, and a thief. But he saw those wagons and knew what the savage voices planned. He couldn't get away, he knew he couldn't make it, not on this sorry nag, but he could at least give a warning. Old Man Duggan leaned forward and jabbed his thumbs into the long ewe-neck. And upstairs, the Big Bookkeeper marked a credit for Aloysius Duggan.

The bay mare jumped her length, jerking the rawhide lead rope from a savage hand. The bay mare stretched her ewe-neck. Long hip muscles bunched and rippled. The bay mare broke through and went downhill. Yells went up. A shot sounded. Arrows *hissed* and ponies broke to run as Apache whips fell. But what was this? The bay mare gained, the bay mare opened distance. The ewe-neck was straight now and stretched, the nostrils flared, the long, flat legs opened and closed like scissors cutting cloth. But this was distance that they cut, twenty-four feet at a stride. The bay mare had been stolen down in Mexico, a sorry nag, brought along to be butchered when the time came. But she would never be butchered now.

Down on the flats the wagons stopped in a hastily formed circle and from that circle little puffs of smoke appeared. The bay mare struck the flats and now she really ran, and Old Man

Duggan, bent flat against her neck, lifted a hoarse voice.
" 'Paches. 'Paches. Look out! They're comin'."
Over in the west, the dust cloud grew.

IV

"RIFLES FOR RED KILLERS"

It took Dandy Bob Roberts just twenty-four hours to reach Tucson. His travel during the night was unmolested, and in the morning, drawn and red-eyed, he changed horses at Pajaritos and rode on. That evening found him stabling his horse and taking his rest in a wagon yard. In the morning he went about his business and, as he talked, only half his mind was on his work. A disturbing thing had happened on the trip to Tucson, a thing that Bob could not explain.

Below Tucson, thirty miles from town, Bob Roberts had found tracks. He had not been following any road but had been cutting across country when he had discovered this sign. Bob was not an expert trailer; he could not, as the saying goes, "track a lizard across a rock", but he was fair enough. There, in hard sand, he had seen the tracks of broad-tired wagons and narrow-footed mules. He had followed them. Presently the tracks of unshod horses had come in from the west, paralleling the wagon tracks. Bob had come to a spot where men had dismounted and in the confusion of sign he had made out that both moccasined men and boot-shod men had been present. Then the horse tracks swept away, again toward the west, and the wagon tracks went on to the stage road. Bob Roberts had those tracks in mind as he moved about Tucson, visiting wholesale liquor dealers, buying wagons and mules, and interviewing men.

There was no trouble concerning the liquor, the wagons,

or the mules. All these were for sale and available, but hiring men was different. Past association made Bob fully conversant with the Old Pueblo's tough nuts and he wanted tough men with him, but most of those he approached wished no part of driving freight through Apache country.

Bob hired four men, and one of those he didn't want. Buckshot Severs, five times indicted for murder, five times cleared, said that he would go. Manuel Sisneros, suspected of being one of the Mimbrés gang of outlaws, agreed to drive a wagon. Herman Dotmann, stolid and Dutch, said that he was not doing anything that wouldn't keep, and old Dad Purcell announced that he intended to visit Gila City, anyhow. It was Dad that Dandy Bob felt he could do without. Purcell had been a buffalo hunter and drifted down to the Old Pueblo from the plains country. He shook with palsy and carried a muzzle-loading rifle that he loaded with round ball. He had been a good man in his day, but now his day was over. Still, he could ride a wagon. Looking at Dad Purcell, Dandy Bob wished that he had brought Duggan along.

Bob was still searching for men when Wilsey Lea found him.

"Hear you're takin' some freight to Gila City, Roberts," Lea said briskly. "That right?"

Bob eyed his questioner narrowly. "That's right," he agreed. "Two loads."

"I'm pullin' out myself in the mornin'," Lea drawled. "Which way you goin'?"

"Stage road, I guess. There's a cavalry patrol down that way. Looks like it would be best."

"Uhn-huh. Got men enough?" There was just a tinge of superiority in Lea's voice.

Bob rose to it. "Plenty," he assured. "Enough to go through all right."

"That's good." Lea turned away. "Maybe I'll see you on the road."

"Maybe," Bob returned, and resumed his search. He had no luck, not even after dark when part of Tucson got drunk and reckless.

In the morning, while warehouse men loaded his two wagons, Bob saw Wilsey Lea pull out of town. There were three big wagons, each with a trailer, each pulled by ten teams, a driver on each wagon, a helper on each trailer. Besides these, Lea had two men besides himself, a compact, well-organized outfit, strong enough, barring complete surprise, to drive off the ordinary Apache raiding crew. Nine hard-shooting men, forted up in wagons, could take care of a lot of Apaches. Dandy Bob wished that he were as well fixed.

Some two hours after Lea's departure, Dandy Bob left Tucson. Severs drove one wagon, with Dad Purcell riding on the seat; Sisneros and Dotmann formed the crew of the other outfit. Having no trailers, Bob's wagons were drawn by six teams each, the driver riding the nigh wheel mule and handling the jerk-line, the helper handling the brake. They creaked down Tucson's street and, entering open country, strung out along the stage road.

Fortune favored them. All through the long, hot day they rolled along in their own dust, and, as night approached and they reached a camping place, they saw wagons ahead, already stopped by water. Bob's outfit rolled in and Wilsey Lea, advancing from the fire, spoke to him.

"I don't know what ailed me yesterday, Roberts. It never struck my mind. There ain't no reason why we shouldn't travel together, is there?"

Suspicion flashed in Bob's mind, but his face was impassive. "We're headed the same place," he said.

"Throw off an' unhitch then." Lea grinned. "We've got coffee made an' stew on the fire. Make yourselves to home."

Dandy Bob dismounted. There was something wrong about this, something queer about the whole deal. Buckshot Severs thought so, too. Trust a murderer to be suspicious!

"What's on his mind, Bob?" Buckshot asked as he bent to unhook his leaders.

"I don't know," Bob admitted. "Keep your eyes open." He went on to pass the warning to Manuel. No use to speak to Dad Purcell.

Teams were unharnessed, watered, and staked out to grass. Bob and his men ate of the stew and drank coffee, made welcome by Lea's crew. Severs stayed close to Bob, with Manuel hovering in the background. Dad Purcell stuffed his pipe and lit it, then, securing lead, a ladle, and a mold from his bedroll, sat by the fire.

"Ain't got no balls for my gun," he observed. "Better cast a few." Lead melted in the ladle over the coals. Purcell smoked the mold and made the castings, dropping his lead balls into water. "Twenty to a pound," he announced. "Man gits one of these things in his gizzard, he knows he's got something." Dad finished his work, cooled his tools, and replaced them.

Weary men went to bed while Lea posted a horse guard.

"No need of you puttin' a man on," he informed them. "One's enough."

"We'll take our turn," Bob replied. "I like to have everybody awake before light comes. Apaches don't move at night, but look out in the mornin'!"

Lea nodded. "Suits me," he agreed.

The night passed without incident. Bob, rousing at three, wakened Severs. Before dawn streaked the sky, everybody was up and alert. Breakfast was eaten, teams watered, harnessed, and hitched to the wagons. The two outfits pulled out together.

Five miles down the road, Lea joined Dandy Bob. "There's a turn-off ahead," he said. "Saves ten miles. We always take it. OK?"

Into Bob Roberts's mind flashed the picture of the broad tire tracks, the tracks of unshod ponies, the sign of moccasins and boots intermingled. Into his mind, too, flashed that ugly rumor. Apaches with new guns, modern repeaters. Lea's two outriders had dropped back with him. Lea's eyes were narrow-lidded, half-hidden.

"Did you take the cut-off comin' up?" Bob drawled.

"I always take it," Lea answered. He rode beside Bob. Beyond him, between Lea and the wagon, rode his two out-riders. Buckshot Severs sat his nigh wheeler, the shotgun that gave him his name across his saddle pommel.

"Buck!" Bob called.

Severs turned his head, lifting it inquiringly. That was all Bob Roberts wanted.

"So did I take the cut-off, Lea," he said. "I saw your tracks an' I saw where they met you. Got the guns this trip?" He moved up as he spoke, his head going down for his Colt.

Lea was not taken by surprise. He did not match Bob's movement; there was no need. Wilsey Lea and his two men had come back to kill Bob Roberts and Lea's gun was already in his hand, drawn, hidden from Bob by Lea's horse. The gun came up. There was a flash, a roar, and Bob's horse went down. As he fell, Dandy Bob Roberts fired three times into that smoke, centering on Wilsey Lea. Behind Bob, Severs's shotgun exploded twice.

Bob scrambled up. Lea's horse ran wild and Wilsey Lea lay on the ground. Beyond him was a man pinned by a horse, victim of Severs's shotgun blast. Past struggling man and horse, another horse and rider moved. The rider swayed in the saddle, toppled, and fell. The wagons were stopped. Buckshot Severs cursed as he scrambled down from his saddle, cursed as he shoved brass shells into the reeking breech of his gun. Manuel and Dad Purcell came running. From Lea's wagons came other men, alarmed, frightened, weapons in their hands. Wide-legged, flanked by Severs, backed by Purcell, Manuel Sisneros, and Dotmann, Dandy Bob Roberts faced these men.

"Hands up!" he snapped. "Drop them guns!" His long-barreled Colt wove a little, circling pattern. Severs's shotgun, Dad Purcell's muzzleloader, Manuel's rifle, Dotmann's rifle, echoed the command. "Drop 'em an' stan' still!"

Slowly men lowered their weapons, letting them slide down to fall on the sand. Slowly hands were raised.

"Lea ain't dead," Manuel announced.

Bob Roberts, gun dangling, walked to the man he had shot. Wilsey Lea's eyes were open. His lips twitched into a mockery of a smile. Bob bent close.

"You'll never make it through," Lea gasped. "You'll . . . never . . . make. . . ." His breath broke on a little soughing gasp.

"Done gone." Severs spoke beside Bob. "Why was it, Bob? I seen him throw up his gun, an' I seen them other two. But why?"

"Meant to kill us," Bob answered briefly. "He's been haulin' guns to sell to the Apaches. Figured to get our loads of liquor, too. Come on an' we'll find out."

Manuel, Purcell, and Dotmann kept teamsters and roustabouts under surveillance while Severs and Dandy Bob lifted a dead horse and rescued the man pinned beneath it. That man, under pressure, talked. He was Carlos Piña, of unsavory reputation, and he talked to save his life. Yes, Wilsey Lea had meant to kill Roberts, as well as his drivers. The wagons were to be burned after their loads had been cached. In the second of Lea's wagons were fifteen rifles, all new guns. It had all been arranged. Oso Rojo's Apaches would meet the wagons at Salado Wash and exchange gold for the weapons.

Bob and Severs looked at each other. "That's what he meant when he said we wouldn't make it." Bob nodded grimly toward the place where Lea's body lay. "He figured on the Apaches. We'll fool him. We'll give 'em the guns, an' they won't touch us."

"Not me," Severs growled. "I'm no good, Roberts, but I don't give guns to Apaches."

"You'll give 'em these guns," Dandy Bob said levelly. "Or I will, after I've plugged the barrels. Dad, you build a fire an' get your lead ladle out. Manuel, you an' Herman pick up the guns these men have dropped. Buck an' me'll watch 'em."

Buckshot Severs grinned and swung his shotgun. "Lead in the barrels," he crowed. "Guess that ought to do it. All right, Manuel, I've got 'em covered."

For a time there was bustling activity. Sullen men stood by under the menace of Severs's shotgun. Purcell built a fire, put on the ladle filled with lead. Manuel and Herman, having searched each teamster, each roustabout, piled weapons on Severs's wagon, brought bright new guns from Lea's wagons. Lea's horse and the horse of Lea's second guard were caught and led in. The saddle was stripped from Bob's dead horse.

"She's melted," Purcell announced.

It was Dandy Bob who poured lead into the new guns. Severs held them and Bob tipped the ladle gently and watched the bright metal trickle down the barrels. Fifteen guns, brass mounted, .45-70s, Winchester repeaters of the latest pattern. When each had been treated, the breech was opened and Bob looked into the barrel.

"Plugged solid," he stated. "Hope the Apaches don't think of that."

Buckshot Severs grunted. "There never was an Indian that knew how to take care of a gun," he said. "They won't. Anyhow, it's a chance we got to take. What about these jaspers, Bob? Kill 'em?" He spoke of Lea's teamsters.

Dandy Bob considered a moment, then shook his head. "Start 'em walkin'," he said. "Head 'em back for town."

Severs considered that, then grinned. "Well, maybe our friends will get 'em," he said. "All right, we'll start 'em walkin'."

The teamsters, informed of what would happen if they looked back, were started on their long walk back to town. Six men trudged off through the sand while Manuel watched them with his rifle.

"Now," Bob said, "let's go. Dad, you drive a wagon. Herman, you drive one. I'll drive one myself. That makes it come out right. Five men, five wagons. An' I hope Oso Rojo is on hand at Salado Wash. I want to get this over with."

Loose horses were tied to wheel horse hames, wheel horses were mounted, and the wagons moved.

Dusk had almost come when Roberts and his wagons reached Salado Wash. Oso Rojo was waiting there, four half-naked bucks with him. Evidently Wilsey Lea had forbidden the Apache to bring more. He rode out to meet the wagons, right hand raised, palm forward in the old plains sign of peace, and Dandy Bob, on the lead wagon, checked his teams.

Oso Rojo spoke a bastard Spanish, capable of interpretation. He was curious. He wished to know the whereabouts of Wilsey Lea. Bob, whose own Spanish was good, made answer. Lea, he said, could not come, but he—and here he tapped his chest—had brought the guns. Had Oso Rojo brought the gold?

It was, Bob knew, touch and go. There were only five Apaches in sight, but all about, he was sure, were more hidden in the wash, secreted behind the rocks and brush. If Oso Rojo was dissatisfied, if he gave a signal. . . .

Oso Rojo grunted that he had brought gold. Where were the guns?

The guns were brought out. Oso Rojo counted them carefully and dumped a *clinking* buckskin bag on the ground. There was the payment, he said, and he needed more guns. He would pay for ten guns more and he would be at this spot to get them. When could these guns be brought to him?

Dandy Bob breathed more easily. If more guns were wanted, then for the moment he was safe. He shook his head, appearing to consider, then counted on his fingers and held up his hands. Eight days, he said. Eight days and he would bring the guns.

Oso Rojo grunted agreement. Bob picked up the buckskin sack. The five Apaches, each carrying three new weapons, mounted three ponies and rode off.

"We'll keep travelin'," Dandy Bob Roberts stated. "We'll keep right on goin' until we're away from here. At that, we're safe enough. They'll never look at those guns tonight."

V

"YELLOW-LEGS"

The wagons kept traveling. For three hours they pulled through the dusk and gathering night. Then, almost back to the stage road, they stopped.

"Two days will see us into Gila City," Bob prophesied. "Just a little luck an' we'll make it."

"We'll make it," Buckshot Severs stated, bending over his frying pan. "Hell, with luck like yours, nothin' will stop us. I'll take first guard, Bob."

Severs took first guard, Herman Dotmann the second, Manuel the third. Bob relieved Manuel and let Dad Purcell sleep. Old Dad Purcell with his shaking hands and his muzzle-loading gun! He'd come in handy. The mules had been left harnessed, and, when dawn broke, the camp stirred. Tugs were hooked and teams strung out. The five wagons moved across the flats.

They reached the stage road and followed it where it ran a quarter of a mile south of a long ridge. The whole world seemed at peace, bathed in the autumn sun. Then, high and quavering, a yell sounded from the ridge, followed instantly by whoops and the sound of shots. From the ridge a rider came pounding down, his horse at a long run, and behind that rider twelve Apache bucks were strung out.

Bob Roberts swung his teams, pulling into a circle, checked his horses, and sprawled down on the wagon top. He squinted over rifle sights and closed his finger on the trigger. Then his head came up.

"Hold it!" yelled Dandy Bob Roberts. "The man in the lead is Duggan!"

There was a gap between the wagons, and Duggan, on the bay mare, came thundering in. Shots, deliberate, spaced, reached out for the Apaches. These, dropping to the sides of their horses, began a circle about the wagons. Peerless horsemen, peerless bowmen, the Apaches. Arrows flickered in the sunlight. A horse screamed and went down, kicking in the harness. Dandy Bob Roberts was on the ground.

"Cut me loose an' give me a gun!" Old Man Duggan rasped. "Cut my feet loose!"

Bob's knife flashed and Old Man Duggan tumbled down. The knife moved again and his hands were free. Herman Dotmann came running from a wagon, bearing a spare rifle, one acquired from a Lea man.

Duggan crouched beside a wheel and fired and worked the lever.

"Damn' Injuns!" Old Man Duggan grunted. "Think they. . . ." He fired again and a horse went down, the rider crawling off like a crazy bug.

Bob's rifle spoke and the crawling ceased. "Where the hell did you come from?" Bob demanded.

"Hell," said Old Man Duggan simply, and meant it.

Outside the wagons, the circle broke. Apaches galloped back toward the ridge. Simultaneously, from Dad Purcell and Manuel Sisneros, yells went on.

"They're pullin' out!"

"Here comes the cavalry!"

Old Man Duggan stood up, peered around the end gate of a wagon, and swore. "Got a drink, Bob?" he demanded. "Say, ketch that mare. I want that mare, I do." Beyond the wagons, riders pounded past, blue-clad men whose blue was hidden by dust.

"In the wagon," Bob Roberts directed. "I'll get some out. You earned a drink, Duggan."

The cavalry lieutenant, returning with his troopers from fruitless pursuit, found six men in the wagon enclosure, passing a bottle around. They offered him a drink, but he refused. He was young and tanned and he wanted to know. The six men told him.

"So you broke free when you saw the wagons?" the lieutenant said, staring at Duggan. "You didn't have a chance, you know."

"I'm here, ain't I?" Duggan demanded, returning the stare.

The lieutenant nodded and stared more intently. "Aren't you the man our scouts chased into camp?" he asked. "I thought I recognized you."

Old Man Duggan winced, then felt Bob's hand on his shoulder. "Duggan," Dandy Bob said, "never runs from Apaches except at exactly the right time. Ain't that so, boys?" Four men nodded solemnly, and Bob Roberts spoke again. "How come you're in this country, Lieutenant?"

"Road patrol," the officer answered briefly. "We jumped Oso Rojo's band this morning, and they stood and fought for a while. Queer thing, too. They seemed to have a great deal of confidence. They were armed with rifles, but only a few of them worked. When they ran, we found fourteen guns, every one new, and every one with the barrel burst or mushroomed. We followed on for a distance but lost them. Then we came back to the road."

"An' a good thing for us, too," Dandy Bob said. "Fourteen guns, you say?"

"Fourteen," the lieutenant repeated.

Around the little circle, eyes met eyes. The officer spoke. "We're returning to Gila City. We'll escort you as far as Lapp Well."

"We'll camp at Lapp Well tonight," said Dandy Bob. "We'll like your company."

The officer and his sergeant left. Men climbed back on wheel horses. Duggan, limping, helped Dandy Bob catch the ewe-necked mare and fasten the rawhide lead rope to the hames of the off-wheel horse.

Dandy Bob, deserting the saddle on the nigh-wheeler, climbed to the wagon top beside Duggan, and the wagon started, flanked by the cavalrymen.

"So," said Dandy Bob, "you run away from the scouts, did you?"

"I was lookin' for you," said Duggan. "Yeah. I run away from 'em." The wheels *creaked* and Duggan talked, telling the truth, mainly, and, when he was finished, it was Bob Roberts's turn.

"What'll you do when we get in?" Duggan demanded when Bob was done. "What'll you do with Quentin?"

"Throw it in his face," Bob answered grimly. "That's what I'll do. Him an' Lea was pardners."

Duggan nodded thoughtfully. Partners stood together, in good or evil. Old Man Duggan understood that. Look at him and Dandy Bob Roberts!

Lapp Well was reached at sundown and camp was made, two separate camps, the military and the civilian. Bob spoke briefly to Buckshot Severs, to Manuel Sisneros, to Herman Dotmann, and to Dad Purcell. They nodded their agreement. What they knew was not a thing for the Army. Their knowledge was their own and they would act on it.

Bob walked over to the soldiers' fire. "Lieutenant," he

said, "we got some fixin's on the wagons that would maybe help out government rations. If the sergeant an' a couple of men would come over . . . ?"

The officer, young but seasoned, grinned understandingly and nodded. "Sergeant," he ordered, "go with this man."

The sergeant and a trooper followed Dandy Bob. They returned, laden, and, if there was a bottle or two in the load, who can say? Certainly not the officer, for he turned his back and walked away. What shoulder bars don't see, they do not know.

"We'll have a guard all night," the sergeant said before he left.

They slept that night, peacefully and undisturbed, and in the morning, still with the troopers accompanying them, went on their way. From Lapp Well to Gila City was twelve miles and six of these were accomplished. Then, ahead of the wagons, a trooper, riding point, threw up his hand and halted. The others came up and joined him. The wagons rolled up and stopped, the drivers climbing down. Blue-clad men made way for them.

"Do you know this man?" the lieutenant demanded, pointing.

Dandy Bob, Duggan, the others, clustered around the body. Ladd Quentin lay, face upturned to the sky. He had not been scalped, but his body was mutilated by many cuts and filled with arrows. Beside the body lay a new Winchester .45-70, its barrel mushroomed.

"Man named Quentin," Bob said.

"I wonder why they didn't scalp him?" the lieutenant said.

"Because," quavered Dad Purcell, plainsman, buffalo hunter, who knew Indians, "they wanted his sperrut to keep livin'. Scalp a man, you kill his sperrut . . . leave his scalp an' his sperrut lives. Laws, but they must've hated him, fixin' him

215

that-a-way. Injuns believe the sperrut is just like the dead man. Look how they cut his arms an' legs."

The lieutenant looked at Dandy Bob Roberts. "Will you put him on a wagon and take him in?" he asked.

"No," said Dandy Bob.

There was that in Bob Roberts's voice that forbade argument. The officer hesitated an instant, then turned. "We'll bury him here, Sergeant," he stated.

"Let's go," said Dandy Bob, and moved to his wagon.

The wagons rolled along. Looking back from the top of their load, Bob Roberts and Old Man Duggan could see troopers digging a grave.

"I guess," Bob said, "I won't throw it at him, Duggan. He come out to meet Lea, an' Oso Rojo caught him. Thought he was me, likely. Thought he was the man that sold 'em those plugged guns. We looked a lot alike, folks said."

Duggan nodded gravely. "That's likely it," he agreed. "What are you goin' to do with the money you got for the guns, Bob? Keep it?"

"No." Dandy Bob shook his head. "I'm going to split it among the boys, Buckshot an' Dad an' Manuel an' Herman. They earned it."

"Yeah," Duggan agreed, "but where do you an' me come in?"

For a time Bob pondered that question. Then: "I don't think anybody will claim Lea an' Quentin's stuff," he said. "I don't know and I don't care. It'll have to go to court for settlement an' we can't get at it. But two of these wagons belong to us, that was part of the deal, an' whoever claims the freight in the other wagons is goin' to pay us for haulin' it. I think, if we play it smart, we can get the teams an' wagons, too. That gives us a freightin' outfit, an' freightin' pays good. Especially when the Apaches are out. We ought to do all right."

"Yeah," Duggan agreed absently, hardly heeding Bob. "Yeah, that's right."

"What have you got on your mind?" Bob asked sharply, noting his partner's preoccupation. "What devilment are you figurin' on now?"

"No devilment," Duggan refuted. "You know me, Bob. I wouldn't start a thing. Only that mare. . . ."

"What about the mare?" Bob demanded.

"Why," said Duggan, "not much. Only that mare c'n outrun her shadder. She's jest got wings, I'm telling you. You seen her come down off the hill. You an' me c'n take that mare an' make some money, Bob. We c'n go over to Yuma an' race her. An' after we clean out Yuma, there's Oro Grande an' Phoenix an' Silver City an' Lordsburg. I tell you, Bob, there jest ain't no tellin' what we c'n do with that mare."

With a flourish, Old Man Duggan produced a bottle filched from the load, and took a long drink.

About the Author

Bennett Foster was born in Omaha, Nebraska, and came to live in New Mexico in 1916 to attend the State Agricultural College and remained there the rest of his life. He served in the U.S. Navy during the Great War and was stationed in the Far East during the Second World War, where he attained the rank of captain in the U.S. Air Corps. He was working as the principal of the high school in Springer, New Mexico, when he sold his first short story, "Brockleface", to *West Magazine* in 1930 and proceeded to produce hundreds of short stories and short novels for pulp magazines as well as *The Country Gentleman* and *Cosmopolitan* over the next three decades. In the 1950s his stories regularly appeared in *Collier's*. In the late 1930s and early 1940s Foster wrote a consistently fine and critically praised series of Western novels, serialized in *Argosy* and Street & Smith's *Western Story Magazine*, that were subsequently issued in hardcover book editions by William Morrow and Company and Doubleday, Doran and Company in the Double D series. It is worth noting that Foster's early Double D Westerns were published under the pseudonym John Trace, although some time later these same titles, such as *Trigger Vengeance* and *Range of Golden Hoofs*, appeared in the British market under his own name. Foster knew the terrain and the people of the West first-hand from a lifetime of living there. His stories are invariably authentic in detail and color, from the region of fabulous mesas, jagged peaks, and sun-scorched deserts. Among the most outstanding of his sixteen previously published Western novels are *Badlands* (1938), *Rider of the Rifle Rock* (1939), and *Winter Quarters* (1942), this last a murder mystery within the setting of a Wild West show touring the western United States. As a storyteller he was always a master of suspenseful and unusual narratives.

THE
MEXICAN SADDLE

BENNETT FOSTER

Trail partners Jim and Waco have only a hundred dollars between them. Then Jim lends *that* to another ranch hand, who leaves him an old Mexican saddle as security. The next day, the ranch hand's body is found, mutilated, his hands tied behind his back. Suddenly, Waco runs into a ranchman who wants very much to buy Jim's saddle. Waco sells it to him, only to find soon enough that it isn't Jim's saddle the ranchman wanted after all, but the Mexican saddle Jim had been given as security. Now it seems like a whole lot of people want that saddle. But why? And why are they willing to kill for it?

- -

ED GORMAN

THE LONG RIDE BACK

For nearly two decades Ed Gorman has consistently provided some of the finest Western fiction around. His ability to create living, breathing characters and his unerring talent for suspense and drama have resulted in stories and novels that no fan of the Old West could ever forget. Now, finally, eighteen of his best stories are collected in one book, eighteen gems that demonstrate the art of storytelling at its peak. Included in this collection is "The Face," the story that won the prestigious Spur Award from the Western Writers of America. No one writes like Ed Gorman, and nowhere is his artistry better displayed than in these exciting tales.

Dorchester Publishing Co., Inc.
P.O. Box 6640   ___5227-X
Wayne, PA 19087-8640 $5.99 US/$7.99 CAN

Please add $2.50 for shipping and handling for the first book and $.75 for each additional book. NY and PA residents, add appropriate sales tax. No cash, stamps, or CODs. Canadian orders require an extra $2.00 for shipping and handling and must be paid in U.S. dollars. Prices and availability subject to change. **Payment must accompany all orders.**

Name: _____

Address: _____

City: _____ State: _____ Zip: _____

E-mail: _____

I have enclosed $_____ in payment for the checked book(s).

For more information on these books, check out our website at www.dorchesterpub.com.
_____ *Please send me a free catalog.*

ED GORMAN

GUN TRUTH

Tom Prine figured that a stint as deputy in a backwash town like Claybank would give him a nice rest. Until, in the space of just a few days, arson, kidnapping and murder turn Claybank into a dangerous place Prine no longer recognizes. Secrets are revealed and at their core is a single nagging question—is anybody in town who they pretend to be? The townspeople claim they want Prine to clear up the mystery, but do they really? And are the people who swear they are his friends in fact the people who are trying to kill him? Prine doesn't have long to find the answers to these questions before the killers move in and make him just one more victim.

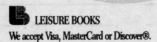